A Candlelight Ecstasy Romance®

"I TOLD YOU I LOVED YOU, AND YOU DUMPED ME," BRIAN SAID ANGRILY.

"That's not so," Diane answered, trying not to attract the attention of the other people at the party.

"Oh? Then suppose you tell me what is. All I know is that I made a real fool of myself over you. You never cared for me at all."

Tears welled up in Diane's eyes. "I don't want to talk to you when you're acting this way."

"Oh, I see. You want me to pretend that everything's fine. Is that it?"

"Get out of my way, Brian. I'm leaving!"

"Isn't that just like you? Whenever things get tough, you just split."

CANDLELIGHT ECSTASY CLASSIC ROMANCES

CANDLELIGHT ECSTASY ROMANCES®

THE SCOUNDREL'S KISS

Joan Grove

A CANDLELIGHT ECSTASY ROMANCE®

Published by
Dell Publishing Co., Inc.
1 Dag Hammarskjold Plaza
New York, New York 10017

*Special thanks to H. Watts, and to John Collins for all
his faith and guidance.*

Dell ® TM 681510, Dell Publishing Co., Inc.

Candlelight Ecstasy Romance®, 1,203,540, is a registered
trademark of Dell Publishing Co., Inc., New York, New York.

ISBN: 0-440-17641-7

Printed in the United States of America

December 1986

10 9 8 7 6 5 4 3 2 1

WFH

To Our Readers:

We have been delighted with your enthusiastic response to Candlelight Ecstasy Romances®, and we thank you for the interest you have shown in this exciting series.

In the upcoming months we will continue to present the distinctive sensuous love stories you have come to expect only from Ecstasy. We look forward to bringing you many more books from your favorite authors and also the very finest work from new authors of contemporary romantic fiction.

As always, we are striving to present the unique, absorbing love stories that you enjoy most—books that are more than ordinary romance. Your suggestions and comments are always welcome. Please write to us at the address below.

Sincerely,

The Editors
Candlelight Romances
1 Dag Hammarskjold Plaza
New York, New York 10017

THE
SCOUNDREL'S
KISS

CHAPTER ONE

With a purposeful air and a quick stride Brian Scott walked across the marble floor of the apartment lobby. Just as he reached the elevator the doors started to close. Clutching his jacket, which was slung over his shoulder, and holding a briefcase, he lunged forward, trying to prevent the inevitable. He was a second too late and the doors snapped shut in his face.

"Damn!" he muttered, and immediately glanced at his Rolex watch.

Terrific! He was already fifteen minutes late for his first meeting with an important client, the prestigious Stephen Wilding. Tardiness might prove fatal, since making a good first impression on the meticulous Wilding was essential to establishing a good working relationship with him.

Brian frowned as he stared at the elevator doors, recalling the frustrating events of the day. All his clients had been annoyingly late, throwing his well-organized schedule into complete turmoil. Trying to make up for lost time, he had rushed from one appointment to another. The brutal humidity of New York City had made his lightweight business suit feel like one large wet noodle.

Brian shrugged and set down his briefcase. He decided it was in his own best interest to try to relax. The damage had already been done, he reasoned, so there was no use worrying about it. Besides, stress only made him feel even more sticky. Even though he was now inside, the air-conditioning afforded little relief. Everywhere in the city, thermostats were set abnormally high because the mayor had imposed energy conservation measures.

Restlessly Brian glanced up at the floor indicator, wondering when an elevator would come down. To his irritation, the car he had just missed was, of course, heading to the top floor, and the only other car appeared to be stuck on the fifteenth floor.

Almost at his wit's end, Brian looked aimlessly around the building's entrance. He could well understand why the affluent Wilding had chosen this place to live. Its ambience reflected a good taste rarely seen these days. A crystal chandelier hung from the high ceiling, and the walls were marbled. To his right, matching ornate gold leaf sconces framed a Gobelin tapestry with an eighteenth-century French table and two chairs beneath.

The sound of heels across the marble floor made him turn. Directly opposite him were rows of mailboxes, and a young woman had walked over to them. His first instinct was to look away, but for some reason, she held his attention. Her hair was auburn, done in an upsweep. She was above average in height—or so her high-heel shoes made her appear—and dressed in a conventional gray suit. A blue tie peeked ever so slightly from her neck. He supposed those frilly, floppy ties were the style now, but he didn't like them. Her appearance was too old-fashioned for his usual taste, but she seemed to be a businesswoman and that appealed to him.

His eyes followed the woman's every move. She unzipped her purse and took out some keys. As she leaned over slightly to open her mailbox, Brian's eyes were attracted to her legs. He was a "leg" man and he sized them up as perfect. They were thin and shapely —the calf had a sinuous curve leading to a trim ankle.

He studied her as she turned in profile. She flipped through the mail; her long, slender hand hinted at an exciting, sensitive touch. She ripped one envelope open and quickly scanned the contents. His curiosity was piqued when he noted the wrinkle forming on her smooth brow. Had the letter brought bad news? he wondered. As if in response to his unspoken question, she abruptly folded the letter, inserted it back into its envelope, and slipped it into her pocket.

She raised her head sharply as if she sensed his scrutiny, but before he could look away, she turned around, then stood there motionless, staring at him. Her blue eyes were bold, yet frightened and vulnerable, and he wondered whether he had offended her in any way. There was something about those eyes, something alive and expressive that contradicted her conservative appearance and suggested the prospect of an erotic experience. It was suddenly clear to Brian why he had been drawn to her: her beautiful eyes, implying intimacy, had given him the answer. He had felt that undefinable and inexplicable impact of human chemistry, and this sudden physical reaction had drawn him like a magnet.

Her startled glare disappeared and was replaced by a look of warning. Perhaps she hadn't approved of his intrusion into her privacy, but Brian felt no embarrass-ment. It wasn't his fault that her eyes had captivated him and made him wish to know their secret. They suggested sensuality coupled with a rare innocence.

Wrapped in contemplation of her, Brian was shocked to find that she had moved and was walking directly toward him. His pulse raced. Moisture formed on his temples. It must have been the heat of the day going to his head, not simply a reaction to a woman he had never met, he tried to tell himself.

But as she neared him, even in her tailored suit, blue blouse, and tie, she looked cool. Brian wondered how she managed to look so fresh in the sweltering heat. He knew he must look like something the cat dragged in. He suddenly remembered his jacket and wished that he had it on now, instead of hanging over his shoulder. He wondered what impression he had made on her. He hoped it was a good one.

Diane Morrison did not think very much of the tall, blond Peeping Tom. Determined not to be intimidated by this man with the furtive brown eyes, she boldly held his stare as she walked directly toward him. She couldn't deny his good looks, but she didn't like the way he looked at her. She was used to getting the once-over, but this guy was giving her the "twice-over"!

To her dismay, her new three-inch heels squeaked as she crossed the floor. Diane hated that sound, and it made her feel even more vulnerable. If *only* she hadn't been so impulsive as to buy those high heels during her lunch hour and then wear them home to break them in. Her customary low pumps, which she'd left at the office, would have been a blessing right now.

12

Diane reached the elevator and stood as far away as possible from the man. She eyed him cautiously. He must have had one hell of a day. He seemed hot, his forehead was damp, and his white shirt was wrinkled. He might live in the building, she thought, or judging by his rumpled appearance, he might be some kind of sleazy salesman.

She was thinking about whether she ought to get into the elevator alone with him, when he flashed a bold smile, displaying a perfect set of white, even teeth. He obviously had used this smile many times. It was too automatic, too easy, like that of some headwaiter at a fashionable restaurant, and he had probably devastated a lot of women with it. Under different circumstances, she probably would have been among its conquests, but now his smile only annoyed her. She didn't like to be leered at, the anonymous letter she had just read had disturbed her, and her feet hurt. All she wanted was to be left alone, to be in her apartment and out of her heels.

Not giving him the satisfaction of responding to his little greeting, Diane diverted her eyes toward the elevator doors, letting him know she hadn't appreciated his eyes on her. At least one of the cars was on its way down, and the awkwardness of standing alongside this man would soon be over. To her annoyance, she still felt him looking at her. What could be the guy's problem? Out of the corner of her eye, she stole a glance at him to confirm her suspicion. Didn't he have any pride? Perhaps he'd been locked up somewhere, and she was the first woman he'd seen in a long, long time, Diane thought disgustedly. Well, whatever he was up to, she was going to put a stop to it!

Diane turned her head slowly, her eyes sharp and assessing as she coolly asked, "Do I know you?"

"No, but I wish you did," he replied cheerfully, without missing a beat.

His direct and unexpected remark instantly lowered her guard, and before she could control them, her traitorous lips had offered him a small smile. Instantly she regretted her response as she stared wide-eyed into the stranger's eager face.

"How about a date?" he asked, deciding to throw caution to the wind.

"I don't 'date' strangers," she answered curtly.

"Make an exception—live dangerously," he came back airily, as if he were using his best sales pitch.

He certainly was a tenacious fellow, she noted dryly. "Don't you know when to take no for an answer?" she asked, not knowing what else to say.

"I know when I see an attractive woman," he stated confidently.

Arrogant, too, she mused.

"How do you manage to look so refreshing in all this heat?" he went on to ask. "What's your secret?"

She wanted to ask him how he got the rumpled look but decided against it. Obviously he wasn't easily discouraged, so maybe her best bet was to ignore him completely, Diane thought.

Luckily, the cables on the elevator began to squeak, and Diane turned her attention toward the sound.

It seemed like forever until the elevator doors opened and the passengers began to file out. But then the nagging question returned. Would she be safe with this man? she wondered, then glanced over at him, hoping to find something about him that would give

14

her the reassurance she needed. She took in his tempting, attractive male physique and rugged appearance. His friendly eyes returned her stare.

To her dismay, she found nothing except what she wasn't particularly thrilled to discover. For as much as the stranger annoyed her, she still couldn't resist the appeal of his sexual magnetism. As she studied his lean but muscular form, he slipped his jacket on, his broad shoulders filling the tailored garment. Obviously, he was visiting someone. One simply didn't put on a suit jacket to go home, she told herself.

Then she tried to convince herself that she was only being silly. What was she worrying about, and why was she so concerned about this strange man? Anxious to be home, she didn't want to wait for the next elevator. Besides, he really seemed harmless enough, even though he did tend to leer a bit. With his good looks and smile, she couldn't imagine the guy's having to lurk around hotel lobbies waiting to jump women. Diane suddenly had the urge to laugh at herself, but she checked the smile that was begging to be expressed. She didn't want to give this man any signal he might interpret as encouragement.

The last of the passengers walked by her, and Diane was pleased to recognize one of them, the little, white-haired Mrs. Dempsey. The old woman's eyes sparkled when she saw Diane.

"Hello! And how are you today?" she asked in her unusually loud but warm voice.

"Fine. And yourself?" Diane inquired, always glad to see the cherub-faced woman.

"As good as can be expected. My arthritis is acting up again," she said simply.

It wasn't a complaint but a statement of fact. That's what Diane liked about Mrs. Dempsey. She always found the more positive side to things.

Abruptly Mrs. Dempsey glanced at the tall man standing opposite Diane. To her surprise, the woman's normally pleasant expression tensed and her eyes narrowed. Mrs. Dempsey actually glared up at the blond stranger before gliding quickly past them. Maybe there was something the little woman knew about this man that *she* should know, Diane thought with wonderment.

"Was it something I did?" the man asked lightly.

Diane looked at him and noted the comical look on his face as he watched the old woman walk down the hall. Diane laughed, more out of nervous relief than anything else.

"Maybe she didn't like your looks," Diane said almost without thinking, then immediately covered her mouth in embarrassment.

To her relief and then chagrin, the good-looking man threw back his head and roared with laughter. The deep, rich sound really irked her. The character had actually liked her remark.

Her brow furrowed as she stared at him. It wasn't *that* funny, was what she wanted to say. Instead, her lips puckered, the way they always did when she was confused or irritated, and she remained silent.

She glanced at the now-empty car. She couldn't stall any longer. Besides, if anything happened to her, Mrs. Dempsey had seen her with him and the police would at least know who did it. It was an insane rationale, but Diane was too tired to think of anything better.

16

Frowning, she moved toward the opened doors as the man next to her bent over and picked up his briefcase.

Her step was too slow; the doors had started to close. The man went into action. He stuck his foot out and stopped the doors.

"Having elevator doors slam in my face twice in one day is not my idea of fun," he declared in a deep, cocky tone.

"Thank you," Diane said, and stepped quickly into the waiting car. Politeness was too ingrained in her character for her to be rude.

She walked straight to the back and leaned up against the wall, feigning a calm she didn't feel. She wondered why she had felt so jumpy, almost paranoid. It had to be the strange letter she'd just received in the mail, she reasoned.

But this man standing next to her bothered her, too. Diane wasn't used to men staring at her the way he had done. Not that she wasn't attractive—she knew she *was*—but she didn't kid herself into believing she possessed the kind of beauty that drew men like a magnet. But no one had ever given her the once-over quite like this joker had done, and what disturbed her the most was that no matter what she told herself, she really enjoyed being stared at by those big brown eyes.

"What floor?" he asked, suddenly breaking into her thoughts.

She stared at him absentmindedly, then realized that in her preoccupation she'd forgotten to push the button for her floor. "Oh, seventeen, please."

Diane watched to make sure he pushed the right button. You can't be too careful, she mused silently.

"Thank you," she said, and looked curiously to see

what floor he was going to. To her surprise, he pushed the penthouse button. So this tall, blond Adonis was visiting Mr. Wilding! Mr. Stephen Wilding, the dapper socialite who lived in her building.

The doors closed and the elevator moved as Diane's thoughts drifted to the letter. She wondered who could have sent it to her and why. There was even the possibility that the sender was a neighbor.

"Hot day, isn't it?" he asked, trying to make conversation, and she glanced at him.

"Yes, but it's typical for New York," she returned.

"Where're you from?" he inquired with keen interest.

Diane checked her frown, annoyed that after so many years in the city, people could still detect her midwestern accent.

"Kansas City," she replied flatly, and looked up impatiently at the floor indicator, not wanting to encourage any more conversation.

The sound of his setting his briefcase down on the floor made her look over at him. His large hand reached inside the breast pocket of his jacket. She hoped he wasn't going to smoke. It was *so* hot. Cigarette smoke in the confined space would be the last straw! Instead, he took out a small silver case, the kind used for business cards, she deduced. The man proceeded to open the case and take out a white card. Pleased that she'd guessed right, Diane mused that perhaps she should give up her job at the newspaper to do detective work. Then he closed the container and put it back into his pocket.

"If you need a lawyer, give me a call. My name's

18

Brian Scott, and I'm with Dwyer, Lytle and Maxwell," he declared proudly.

Diane stared at the little white card, not believing her eyes. So the Peeping Tom was an attorney. Wonders never ceased!

Not knowing what else to do, she took the offered card, then muttered, "Thanks."

What an original way of picking up women. She had to give the guy that much, Diane thought as she promptly opened her purse and dropped the card inside.

"And you're . . . ?" he pressed, a strange, faintly eager glint flashing in his eyes.

Diane stared at him stubbornly. She didn't want to give the stranger her name, but she knew she should have thought of that before she'd accepted his card. In doing so, she had given him the perfect opportunity to ask who she was. What could she tell him—that it was none of his business? No, that wouldn't do."

"Diane Morrison," she answered abruptly.

"That has a nice sound to it."

"It does?" she asked, curious as to what this guy would come up with next.

"Morrison's a Scottish name, isn't it?"

"Yes, it is," she confirmed, sure that he was working up to something.

Before the man could say anything further, the car slowed to a stop. To Diane's relief, it was on her floor and she saw her escape. Walking briskly toward the doors, she prepared herself for a quick getaway.

But just as the doors opened, and she was about to step out, he extended his arm in front of her, blocking her exit.

19

"Remember, call me if you need legal advice, and if you don't you can still call me," he told her, his dark, intense eyes underscoring his come-on.

"I'll keep that in mind," she retorted sharply as she quickly slid past him.

He might be gorgeous, but he was still unbelievably arrogant, she mused as she moved out of the elevator and into the hallway.

But the stranger was put out of her mind the instant the doors closed behind her. Diane was tired, and she sighed deeply. It had been a long day. She checked out the long hallway to see if anyone was around. Satisfied there wasn't, she slipped out of her shoes and walked barefoot toward her apartment.

Unlocking her door, she walked into her comfortable, spacious apartment. She dropped her shoes onto a chair and placed her purse on a small chrome table with a glass top next to the door. The stifling heat of the apartment hit her in the face, but Diane hardly felt it. Once surrounded by the security of her home, the problem of the anonymous letter came back to trouble her.

Anxiously she flipped through her mail. Her first assumption had been correct: they were all bills—all except for the strange letter she'd stuffed in her pocket. She took out the envelope and reexamined it. Because of the handwriting on the outside, Diane had known it wasn't a bill and had opened it. But it had not been the piece of correspondence she'd been expecting from a friend. No, it had not been anything even close to that.

Diane stared at the envelope, hoping to discover a clue to the identity of the sender. The handwriting still held no answer for her, nor did the local postmark.

There was nothing unusual about it except that the stationery was very faded and there was no return address. She nervously tapped the envelope against her outstretched hand, wondering what kind of person would send something like that to her.

Turning the envelope over, she pulled out the letter and reread the handwritten words.

You are bright at what you do, but you don't know what's going on in your own backyard. Please look around and put an end to innocent people being preyed upon.

She went over the words a few times, but try as she may, they meant nothing to her. The words "You are bright at what you do" would have to mean her work on the obituary column at the newspaper because she didn't have any hobbies, she thought. Her "backyard" could be where she lived or where she worked. It was all too much for her. None of it made sense, and a headache threatened her overworked brain. The letter had to be a prank, she assured herself, and tossed it down with the rest of her mail.

Feeling a lot more relaxed, Diane realized she was hungry. She turned and headed toward her large, modern kitchen. Thinking she needed a special treat after her trying day, she took a nice, thick filet mignon out of the freezer. Setting it on the counter to thaw, Diane decided she would have a big salad to go with it. With her dinner planned, she felt a lot better. Her only problem now was how to get cool.

Diane walked over to the air conditioner and turned it on high, hoping the machine would work its magic quickly. Even though her commitment of putting her sister through college was now completed, Diane still didn't feel she could afford the luxury of leaving the air conditioner running on full power throughout the day. But hot, sticky days like today made her wish she had.

Diane couldn't wait a minute longer to get out of her constricting clothes. As she got undressed, she found herself wishing that an immaculate appearance wasn't of so much importance to her. Of late the effort was becoming a real drag. And her dissatisfaction with her own formal style of dress was only the tip of the iceberg. It seemed more and more, as the days flew by, that she wasn't really getting a lot out of life, that she wasn't really enjoying herself enough. All her spontaneity had been lost somewhere between the pressures of her office and her pleasant but rather routine social life. Not that she didn't like her work at the newspaper; she thought herself very fortunate to have landed that job. And not that her social life was that bad; it wasn't. She had dated some very nice men. But with all that, Diane had become aware that something was lacking in her life.

She couldn't figure out what had suddenly come over her. She felt more restless than usual, she admitted. Well, maybe it was only the hot weather. She shrugged. Summer always made her yearn for love and a carefree life, neither of which she had. Diane automatically shook her head. On no account was she going to allow herself to dwell upon the fact that she didn't have a special man in her life right now. Her mother would always take care of that for the both of them. Every time she had told her mother she was dating someone new, her mother always mentioned how much she wanted to become a grandmother. Their telephone conversations were always cut short upon reaching that subject, and Diane had soon learned not to discuss her dates with her mom. Diane was a true believer that someday she would find that perfect man. And she could wait.

Now clad only in her bra and panties, Diane gathered up her discarded clothing and moved quickly through her tastefully decorated living room toward her bedroom.

Entering the room, she hung up her clothes and slipped into her blue cotton lace robe. Then deciding a cool shower might help her relax, Diane headed toward the bathroom.

As the refreshing water sprayed over her slim body, Diane suddenly thought of the handsome man she had met at the elevator, and her nerve endings tingled as she recalled his intense, mysterious stare. No man had ever looked at her the way he had, and with the thought of him, goose bumps broke out on her skin. The guy was a real hunk, she thought, and a grin formed on her lips. It made her laugh to think that she, Miss Prim and Proper, would ever use that term, even in her thoughts. But she had, and that's what he was, she mused. Now she had seen in living flesh what all the romantics were sighing about. It was strange that a complete stranger could affect her the way he had, and she found herself wondering if she'd ever see him again. Even though she had told him her name, she wasn't listed in the telephone book. So nothing would ever come of their chance meeting.

But the guy definitely hadn't hidden his interest. His stare had been ample proof of that. Maybe she reminded him of someone—an old girlfriend, a relative, maybe an ex-wife. Diane knew she wasn't any great beauty, so that couldn't be the reason he had been so attentive to her. Ten minutes was all it took to apply her makeup. But that's all it had ever taken to perfect her tailored, businesslike appearance. Perhaps now was the time to do something about her image. Diane had to admit she had grown tired of her present one. She used to be so much more unconventional, so much freer in her dress and life-style. Her style of dress, no doubt, had changed simply because of circumstances. It was a struggle for her to survive in the big city and in the newspaper world. Diane had had to make herself fit into her structured corporate environment. One simply did not rock the boat if one wanted to get ahead.

But her attraction to this guy was something new to her. She tried to recall his name but couldn't. His presence had flustered her so much that she had forgotten. She'd have to take a look at his card to get the alluring hunk's name when she got out of the shower. Diane had to admit to herself that she wanted to see him again. But with that thought she felt strangely vulnerable. Her mixed feelings confused her. She felt pulled strongly toward him, and yet, at the same time, she knew she should stay away from him at all cost. It just didn't make sense to her.

All these thoughts seemed suddenly much too heavy for her, and she wanted to dismiss the handsome stranger from her mind. She turned off the water and stepped out of the shower. As she reached into the cabinet for a towel, she caught a glimpse of her body in her full-length mirror. Her nude body glistened with little drops of water. She thought of how beautiful her stranger's body must be, hidden beneath those business clothes of his. Suddenly Diane was seized with an inexplicable arousal. Oh, if only that man could see her now! What would he do? The answer was obvious.

Brian had already made up his mind that he wanted to see Diane again. There was something about her that excited him. He just had to meet her again and find out what about her was so alluring, he thought as he headed out of the building. His appointment had gone well with Wilding, and it looked like he would have reason to spend some time near her home as the wealthy man's attorney—or he could make up some excuse for being there.

What were his advantages in this game of pursuit? he wondered. First, she had given him her name—Diane Morrison—and that was a start. He would call her and ask her out to dinner. She had refused him once, but he could tell she liked him and he felt it was worth another try. When he got home, he'd call information and get her number. Then the disturbing thought occurred to him that she might not be listed. A lot of women living alone in New York preferred the security of not having their name in the directory. He also didn't know if she was single. He really should try to find that one out, before trying to date her.

Well, he thought with a determined air, he could confront her presumably by chance or run into her. That's what he'd do, he thought smugly as his long legs briskly carried him toward his apartment. He was glad he lived within walking distance. Once he was home, he would look up her number right away.

CHAPTER TWO

Diane sat at her desk and stared stubbornly at the disarray of papers on the mahogany surface. She couldn't work. At first the mysterious letter had bothered her. Then she managed to put it out of her mind only to discover that she had a deeper problem.

The restlessness she had felt the evening before had come back to haunt her. She still didn't have the foggiest idea what was bothering her or even when it had begun. Perhaps there wasn't any specific starting point —only a slow progression. For not only did Diane find her conservative dress restricting and her life too routine, it was also harder for her to concentrate on her work. She just couldn't understand why she didn't feel like working. It was so unlike her almost workaholic nature. Also, there wasn't any real reason for her dissatisfaction. She was comfortable in her job, she made good money, and she liked her boss and coworkers. So what could be the problem?

Her brow furrowed. Diane sighed deeply and leaned back in her chair. Her glance darted aimlessly around the small office, making a trail from the beige lamp to the large green plant, then across her typewriter. She wondered what had come over her. She must be in a rut. That was all. Everything in her life had become too routine. She could practically do her work blind-folded. She needed a challenge. Yes, that was the answer. Boredom had her in its clutches, she thought with a wry grin. Now that she understood her problem, what was she going to do about it?

Standing, Diane walked over to her window. There wasn't much of a view of the city's skyscrapers because her office was only on the seventh floor, but she could see a piece of the sky above the street, squeezed between two tall buildings. The sky was a clear, flawless blue—the kind of sky that made Diane anxious to travel. But a vacation was not in the cards; she needed to do something about her career. And today was as good as any to go in and talk to her boss, John O'Rourke, about a possible change. She'd been in the obit department a long time and felt she needed a challenge. Now that her obligation to her sister was out of the way, she could afford to take a risk by trying something new. Perhaps O'Rourke could find her something in another department. If worse came to worse, she could always try to get a job at another newspaper.

Diane turned abruptly from the window. She felt good about her decision, but she also knew that her boss might not like the idea of her changing jobs. She was good at her work, and she knew that jobs were at a premium at the paper. Maybe she could stay in her position if O'Rourke could arrange some outside reporting for her. After all, while in college, she had majored in journalism, and writing feature articles had been her first love. So much so, that when she came to the city and accepted the job with the *New York Press,* she thought she would be able to work her way up to reporting. Her boss had taken her under his wing and taught her the ropes. Unfortunately the only slot open had been in the obituary department. As time went by, Diane was eventually promoted to editor and became very content with her new position. In a way, she had traded her aspirations for security. But she never complained. She had been happy there at the newspaper, that is, until just recently.

Glancing at her beige phone, Diane thought about dialing her boss's extension. She knew O'Rourke would be offended if she didn't approach the subject in the right way. After all, he had been her mentor. Yes, before Diane talked to him, she would have to give the problem a lot of thought, decide how to handle it in the best way, and figure out the right moment to speak to him. If only she could find the right words to help her boss understand.

Absentmindedly, Diane flipped through the morning newspaper as she mulled over her new dilemma. Suddenly one article caught her eye and she read it. It was about Mr. Wilding. She didn't know him personally, but she'd seen him several times in the lobby of their building. The widower seemed to be a "ladies' man"—always politely bowing and opening the doors for all the women. On one occasion, she had even seen him carrying an old woman's groceries. The wealthy socialite and his glamorous life-style fascinated Diane, but what had really attracted her to the article was that the headline had named Dwyer, Lytle and Maxwell as the new law firm handling Wilding's large holdings. So *that* was the reason for Brian Scott's visit to the penthouse. She smiled when she recalled the tall stranger's name. This time she had no trouble remembering it. She must have looked at his card a dozen times last night.

Diane somehow managed to get through the rest of the day, finishing some of her work. She glanced at her watch. She had arranged to meet with her boss at the end of the working day. It was time for her to go into his office and state her case.

Straightening the papers on her desk as best she could, Diane stood and took her suit jacket off the back of her chair, then slipped into it. She walked slowly toward Mr. O'Rourke's office. She was still worried about how he would take her news, but nothing would stop her from talking to him. She knew she had to. Before her restlessness got any worse, she felt obligated to confide her feelings to her boss. She had a great deal of respect for the man and also considered him to be her friend. As she approached his office her steps quickened.

Just as she reached his door, she straightened her back and squared her shoulders. Diane reached and tapped lightly on his closed door. An uneasiness momentarily came over her, and she sighed deeply, hoping to find him in a good mood. She knew how pressured he felt at times because of the daily deadlines. And she prayed that he would have time for her today.

"Come in," she heard him call, and Diane turned the doorknob, opening the door.

He smiled when she entered, and Diane felt it was a good sign. She smiled in return and looked around the familiar office. Mr. O'Rourke was a theater buff and loved going to Broadway shows. Colorful posters of his favorite plays adorned his otherwise plain office. It was his hobby, and he always looked forward to Diane's noticing the posters and complimenting him on his good taste.

"I see you've got another one. It's stunning," Diane declared, pointing out a particularly pretty multicolored poster.

"Thanks," he said proudly. "Please have a seat, Diane."

She automatically chose the chair directly in front of his desk and studied the man sitting across from her, wondering if he were ill. It wasn't like her boss to pass up an opportunity to discuss his latest theater outing.

"I hope nothing's wrong. You sounded so serious when you called," he continued.

Diane forced a smile. Apparently he had heard the confusion in her voice when she called him this morning. Whenever anything was hard for her to do, she had a way of steeling herself that often warned others of her problem.

"I don't know how to start this," she began nervously.

"Just start anywhere," he encouraged her, folding his hands and leaning back in his chair.

Diane breathed easier as she looked into the little man's kind face. It was just like him to encourage her to speak her mind, regardless of the consequences. She realized that most of her anxiety had more to do with her own feelings of insecurity than with any real fear of what her boss might say or do.

"I want to talk to you about my job, and I—"

"I know you've been a little overworked lately," he interrupted.

"That's true, but that's not why I wanted to talk to you, John. . . . When you first hired me, I took the job because I thought it was a good opportunity to learn the business. And you taught me everything I know—you've helped my career all along the way. But I've been in my present position for almost three years now, and I wondered whether there might be an opening in some other department."

Diane breathed deeply, relieved she had gotten it all out, and then waited for his reaction as she stared wide-eyed into his face.

John's ears twitched ever so slightly—the way they always did when he heard something he didn't like. Diane tensed, bracing herself for the worst.

"I'm totally surprised. I had no idea you were unhappy here," he declared in a somewhat deflated tone.

"It's not that I've been unhappy," she explained. "It's been wonderful working with you. But my work has become too routine, and I feel I need more of a challenge. I just want to do some reporting. I would even be willing to take a cut in salary for the opportunity."

"Diane, I'm sorry, but there's nothing open right now," he said flatly, his features stern.

"Maybe I could do some outside work—work that normally would be given to free-lancers," she suggested, grasping at straws.

"And create problems among your coworkers?" he asked, his brows raised.

She shouldn't have said that, Diane thought, realizing that she was talking to a stone wall.

"No, you know I wouldn't want to do that," she admitted with a sigh of resignation.

"The truth of the matter is, Diane, you do a terrific job. And besides, there isn't any place to move you.

There're a lot of reporters who have more experience than you," he declared honestly.

His words were said kindly enough, but they offered no solace to Diane.

"That's what comes from being too good at what you do," he added with a kind smile.

"Oh, well, it was worth a shot," she stated in a disappointed voice.

"You've been working too hard, Diane. Maybe all you need is a rest. Why don't you take tomorrow off and give yourself a long weekend? That way, you'd come to work refreshed on Monday. It could give you a new outlook. If it doesn't, then we'll talk some more. I'd really hate to lose you, but right now there isn't anything I can do for you," he said warmly as his sincere blue eyes met hers.

"I appreciate that, John, but I can't take tomorrow off. There's just too much to be done here, and there would be even more facing me on Monday morning."

"Why don't you leave some for Ted to do? You have to learn to delegate some of the responsibility?"

Diane grinned sheepishly. Her dear old boss had her number, all right. Being the perfectionist she was, it was always hard for her to believe that someone else would take as much care with a project as she would. And John was right: she *did* need a rest. It had been a long time since she'd taken a day off, and it *was* summer. She needed some time off to clear her head. Perhaps she hadn't given it enough thought before talking to him about getting another job.

"Well, what do you say?" he asked hopefully. "I'll keep my eyes open for a spot for you, even though I don't think there will be anything available for a while. Anyway, take some time and think about it."

"Okay, you've convinced me. I won't be in tomorrow, then. But I won't palm my work off on Ted tonight. It's too late and it wouldn't be fair. I'll stay a little later and get as much done as I can, so it won't all be facing me when I get back."

With her decision made, Diane stood up. She would use the time to decide what she really wanted to do, then see if she really felt the same on Monday. If she did, she might put some feelers out for another job or wait a little while before discussing a job transfer with her boss.

"Have a good weekend," she heard him call after her as she turned to leave.

Her mind was in a whirl, trying to decide what work should be finished and what could be left for Monday.

Brian stood outside the apartment building, discussing every topic he could think of with the superintendent, Mr. Edwards, waiting for Diane to come home. When he got around to the weather, he knew he was hitting the bottom of the barrel.

He felt like a schoolboy with a bad crush, anxious to get a glimpse of his girlfriend. He knew it was ridiculous to stand out there in the heat, expecting Diane to arrive home at the same time as she had the night before. She could have a late appointment—or even a date after work. He knew his chances of running into her were slim, but that didn't bother Brian. What he wanted, he went after and got, and he definitely wanted to see the lovely woman again. Judging by her prim and proper attire, he assumed she was very organized and ran her life on a schedule. If that was so, then he stood a good chance of running into her.

But as he glanced at his watch for the tenth time, he was beginning to doubt his reasoning powers. He might have misjudged her. After all, her eyes had definitely hinted at a different, more spontaneous nature that contradicted the rigid, businesslike image she presented to the world.

Well, it was obvious that he couldn't just stand there and talk to the super all day, but he still had one card up his sleeve. He had the papers to deliver to Wilding. He could have sent them over by messenger, but he decided to bring the documents himself, using them as an excuse to see her again. If luck would have it, maybe he would meet her on the way out of the building.

But not all had been in vain. Brian had learned that Diane wasn't married. The news had made his day. He didn't particularly like that he had to ask the super about her. It went against his normal ethics, but he didn't want to make a fool of himself if she did have a husband, nor had he wanted her to see his disappointment.

Deciding it was time to see Wilding, Brian took one last look in the direction she might walk. His hopes rose as he thought he saw her, and he quickly turned his attention back to Edwards.

As Diane approached her building, she saw her super standing outside with another man. Nearing the building, she suddenly realized that the man was Brian Scott. Her step faltered, and then she walked more quickly as an excitement enveloped her. She was surprised to see him at her building for the second day in a row. Perhaps he had more than one client in this building. It didn't seem likely that he would be visiting Wilding again so soon.

Mr. Edwards, the super, was the first to turn and greet her.

"Hello, Ms. Morrison," he said politely.

"Hello," she replied, and glanced over at Brian.

"Have you met Mr. Scott?" the super asked quickly.

"Yes, I have," Diane replied, smiling.

Brian smiled back at her warmly. She wasn't prepared for the effect he had on her. She had known he was handsome, but the feeling was even more intense than she remembered. There was something clean and refreshing and unusually attractive about his looks. He reminded her of those ruggedly handsome outdoor guys in the cigarette ads.

"Hello, Diane," he said simply.

Her heart was momentarily frozen by the deep, rich sound of his voice. Her feet felt glued to the spot, and her face, locked in a smile, felt like it would surely break. Why hadn't he affected her that way yesterday? she wondered. Then she remembered she'd been preoccupied with the anonymous letter. That must have softened the impact of this man, she decided.

"Have to get back to work," the super suddenly announced, snapping Diane out of her trance.

"It's about time," she teased as the man laughed. Her eyes followed his departure.

For some reason, she did not want to look up into Brian's face. She didn't trust her own expression. She wanted a few moments to regain her composure.

"Fancy running into you," he said lightly.

"Some people are just lucky," she answered flippantly.

He laughed, then said, "You're too much."

"Thank you," she replied demurely.

"I think we'd better stop meeting this way and get together and go out for dinner," he suggested.

Oh, no, not that again, Diane thought with dismay. Then she suddenly wondered just what he was doing out in front of her building. Her eyes narrowed as she gave him a skeptical glance.

"You certainly are persistent," she stated matter-of-factly.

"I come right to the point, if that's what you mean."

"Ah, the direct approach," she replied, a note of sarcasm in her voice.

"Being a lawyer, you learn to state your case as early and as clearly as possible."

"Oh, so now I'm being referred to as a 'case.' "

"That's not exactly what I had in mind," he said in a low voice.

Diane stared defiantly into his eyes. She wondered just what Brian *did* have in mind but couldn't bring herself to ask. He seemed like such a respectable fellow, dressed in his business suit, looking every inch the prosperous attorney. But what was he doing lurking in front of her building?

He certainly had a way of stirring up her nerve endings. Maybe it would be better for her to accept his invitation and find out what he was after, she thought. Despite his decidedly odd behavior, Diane couldn't bring herself to believe he could harm her in any way.

"Are you married?" she asked boldly, wanting to make sure she wasn't letting herself in for trouble.

"No, I'm not. If I were, I wouldn't be asking you out," he stated firmly.

Feeling like he was chiding her as if she were a child, Diane retorted, "But maybe I am."

"I know you're not," he said, in such a confident tone that she almost considered hitting him.

"You sound pretty sure of yourself," she came back, suddenly wondering why she had even considered going out with this arrogant man.

As if picking up on her change of feelings toward him, he smiled boyishly at her, but Diane held firm and glared back.

"I took it upon myself to find out. I hope you don't mind," he said.

Her lips puckered. She wasn't going to let that little-boy routine work on her when she had him dead to rights, she thought with irritation. But he did have a way of affecting her, stimulating her in a way no other man could. Despite her better judgment, she wanted to be with him. She couldn't deny that.

But he had been prying into her personal life, and she wouldn't let him get away with that.

"You asked Mr. Edwards?" she ventured, trying to keep her anger in check.

"Yes, I did," he admitted, nodding.

What annoyed her more than anything else was that he didn't even seem to think he'd done anything wrong.

"I can't believe you would do something like that!" Diane exclaimed angrily.

"I know it wasn't exactly the proper thing to do," he said, slightly taken aback.

" 'Wasn't exactly the proper thing,' " she mimicked,

her anger now out of control. "And I suppose you were hanging out here today, checking up on me!"

The minute the words were out of her mouth, she could have died. She hadn't meant to give voice to her thoughts.

To her astonishment, Brian chuckled.

"I guess I deserved that," he said. "I have to admit I was hoping to see you, but I also have business here."

"You do?" she asked skeptically.

"Yes, I have some papers to drop off to Mr. Wilding," he replied, flashing her a charming smile.

"In the future, if there's anything you want to know, I'd appreciate it if you wouldn't go snooping around my home," she warned, letting him know she wouldn't tolerate that kind of behavior. Then, she added, sternly, "Just ask me."

"You're right and I apologize. Accepted?"

Diane glanced away shyly and then looked back into his serious, earnest face.

"At least I told you the truth. Don't I get some credit for that?"

"I guess I'll have to give you *some* credit for that," she conceded, and couldn't help but smile.

"Boy, I wouldn't want you sitting on my jury," he said lightly.

"The wrong person certainly wouldn't go to jail," she declared, a challenging look in her eyes.

"How about that dinner date?" he asked, not willing to be put off.

"You've got a one-track mind, don't you?"

"Yep."

She looked into his dark brown eyes and noted his long dark lashes. He had the most beautiful lashes she'd ever seen on a man. They were thick and curled up ever so slightly. It was funny, but everything about him seemed to turn her on.

So, what did she have to lose? Everything. He was arrogant and sneaky and made her feel weak in her knees.

"What are you afraid of? I don't bite," he said suddenly, jerking her out of her thoughts.

"Don't you?" she returned without missing a beat.

"What if I told you I'd be on my best behavior?" he asked with an irresistible twinkle in his eyes.

Diane stared stubbornly at the man, trying to make up her mind. She had never before gone out with a man who was essentially a stranger, but her super had validated Brian's credentials, she told herself. Besides, it was hard to stay mad at a guy who had gorgeous eyelashes. And it was about time she did something more spontaneous than she was used to doing.

"All right," she barely whispered.

"Great!"

"When?"

"How about tomorrow night?"

"Okay," she agreed.

"Can I carry that up for you?" he asked, looking at her briefcase.

An awkward smile flashed across her face. She had totally forgotten about the case dangling from her hand.

"Sure," she replied, and handed her briefcase to him.

It had been a long time since anyone had carried a bag for her. But then again, it had been a long time since she had wanted to let anyone do anything for her, she reminded herself.

"That was very nice of you," she said as an afterthought.

"Men should always being doing things for a beautiful woman like you," he murmured.

Beautiful. The man had said she was beautiful. She wanted to tell him he wasn't so bad looking himself, but Diane remained silent as they turned to enter the building.

Stepping into the elevator, Diane couldn't contain her curiosity and asked, "So, you're visiting Wilding again?"

"Yes, do you know him?"

"No, not really. I mean, I see him come and go, but I've never talked to him."

"He's got quite a reputation," Brian declared.

Diane studied his face, waiting for him to explain his remark, but he offered nothing further. She wondered what he meant but decided not to ask him.

Instead, she replied, "I read where your firm is handling his business affairs now."

"Yes, that's true," he stated simply.

"You should be happy about that."

"Yes, looks like I'll be around a lot," he said with a grin.

But Diane's features hardened as she glared at him. She hoped the clown didn't have any ideas about his business trips giving him easy access to her apartment.

"Well, don't knock yourself out," she retorted flippantly.

"What's that supposed to mean?" he asked.

Diane laughed, unable to stay angry at this overwhelmingly appealing man. "Nothing really. What time should I be ready?" she asked, changing the subject.

"How about seven?"

"Sounds good to me."

Brian flashed her one of his irresistibly devastating grins just before the elevator doors opened. Diane returned his smile briefly and slipped out into the corridor.

Once inside her apartment, Diane leaned up against the door. She felt on top of the world. She had taken a big step, a giant step, by accepting Brian's invitation. All the lethargy she had felt earlier had evaporated, and now she was rejuvenated. She was starting anew. Tomorrow would be the first day of the rest of her life.

CHAPTER THREE

Diane lounged in her bed, sipping coffee, listening to her favorite radio station, and catching up on her reading. She felt like a contented fat cat, curled up in a ball. It had been a long time since she'd allowed herself to sleep as late as noon, and it felt wonderful. Maybe there *was* something to the easy life, she mused as she stretched and yawned.

After she finally got out of bed, Diane took a long hot bath. She promised herself that she wouldn't do any housework; she'd relax all day. And as the day wore on, Diane felt more confident that her boss had been right. She needed some rest and fun. She had been under a lot of pressure, and now was the time for her to start enjoying herself.

By early evening, Diane was totally relaxed. But when it came time to get ready for her date with Brian, it was a different story. She couldn't believe herself. Normally she applied her makeup in a matter of minutes. But tonight it took her almost a full hour. She was certainly making an extra effort to look her best. She wanted to laugh at herself but couldn't. The excitement she felt at seeing him again was too strong. She felt excited and yet apprehensive at the same time.

But the desire to be with him outweighed everything else.

Diane paused with makeup brush in hand and stared into the mirror, studying her image. She had to admit the extra effort had worked wonders. Her new look reminded her of the beauty make-overs she'd seen in fashion magazines. But she frowned, realizing it was about time to do something about her hair. Her rather severe-looking upswept hairdo had to go. There was nothing to do about it now, however; it was too long to be worn any other way. Diane decided to get it cut shoulder length as soon as she could make an appointment with her hairdresser. With that decided, she was quite pleased with the new her.

Putting the last touches of powder on her face, she found herself wondering why she hadn't given this much time to her makeup before. What had made the difference? The hunk had made the difference, a small voice from way inside answered. And Diane knew it was true.

It wasn't that she was complaining. It was really wonderful to be excited enough about someone to take that kind of care. But it also made her wonder why she hadn't at least done it for herself before. She always looked neat and very efficient—but never glamorous. Had she been unconsciously sabotaging her looks, deliberately trying to turn men off? That was possible, she thought, even though she hated to admit it. She really liked men and missed having a special one in her life, but perhaps she had been concentrating too much on her career and not enough on her social life. Until recently, she had really had no other choice. Putting all her energies into her work had been essential to acquire the kind of financial success required to support her sister's education. But now she was free once more to live her own life.

Diane's eyes brightened with the thought of her sister Connie. She loved her baby sister and was so very proud of her. Diane never regretted any of her sacrifices to help Connie through school. She had promised her sister she'd always take care of her, and she had kept that promise. After their father had died unexpectedly, it had become quickly apparent that he had failed to provide adequately for his family. On the advice of an accountant, Diane invested the bulk of their father's savings to provide enough money for their mother to live comfortably for the rest of her life. It was mutually agreed upon that whatever was left over would be used to finance Diane's education. So then it was only fair that she would help Connie when the time came.

But with her obligation now finally over, Diane knew it was time to take a good look at her own life. She had to admit that she had allowed herself to hide behind her responsibility to Connie and had used it to avoid any real commitment to anyone. She had always believed she couldn't handle the demands of both her job and a relationship. Perhaps she could have handled both, but Diane just wasn't made that way. She arranged everything in order of priority and completed each task before starting the next.

Now she had the time for a real relationship, and meeting Mr. Scott had made her keenly aware of this. She didn't know anything about his personal life, but he was just too damn attractive not to go out with. Diane wondered idly if the hunk would try to kiss her when he took her home. He seemed like the type who could probably have any woman he wanted, and she didn't want him to think of her as just another conquest. But Diane couldn't deny that she wanted to experience the touch of his lips.

Brushing a bit more of blusher on her cheeks, Diane felt well armed to meet him. Studying her face in the mirror, she knew she was happy that she had accepted his invitation after all.

Later that evening, Diane sat across from Brian in an outdoor café, thoroughly enjoying herself. The sky had become overcast and the balmy air hinted at rain, but the weather held and it turned out to be a beautiful evening.

"I'm really enjoying this," she murmured, feeling very comfortable and looking into Brian's eyes.

"Me, too. I'm so glad you decided to come."

His words were underscored by a warm smile, making Diane feel he was sincere.

"How could I resist? You twisted my arm," she teased.

"What?" he asked in a disbelieving voice, feigning a hurt expression.

"You did. Snooping around and asking people about me," she went on unmercifully.

"I thought you had accepted my apology," he said softly.

A strange seriousness had come over him, making Diane uncomfortable. Perhaps she had hit a nerve.

"You're right, I did," she returned in a more somber tone.

"I really am sorry about that, Diane, and I wouldn't want you to hold that against me," he explained.

"I've forgotten about it. But you do know how I feel. I'm a very private person, and I believe it only right that if you want to know something about me, ask me, not someone else."

"You have very beautiful eyes. Has anyone ever told you that?" he asked, ignoring her words.

"No, you're the first," she teased.

He gave her a skeptical look. Diane couldn't help but wonder why she was being so flippant. It was almost as if she were afraid to take him seriously.

"I'll bet," he retorted.

"A girlfriend of mine told me that was the best answer for that line," she said with a laugh.

"Now you think I'm giving you a line."

Diane laughed again. "I didn't mean exactly that."

"What's the 'exactly' part?"

Diane gave him a me-to-know-and-you-to-find-out look.

"Not going to tell me?" he asked.

"No," she answered smugly.

"I think you have the wrong impression of me."

"How could I? I hardly know you," she replied, curious as to what Brian was getting at.

"I think you're naturally suspicious of men," he responded carefully.

"What makes you say that?" Diane asked, a little too keenly.

"Aha! I'm right, aren't I?"

"What is this, twenty questions?" she snapped, feeling he was trying to dig into her psyche.

"I've hit a sore spot, haven't I?" he asked. When no

answer seemed forthcoming, he said, "I'm sorry. I didn't mean to. Let's drop the subject."

Diane stared into his eyes, noting the look of regret there, and realized that maybe she'd been a little too sensitive.

"No, wait a minute," Diane insisted. "You just opened a can of worms, and I'm not going to be left with the damn wiggling things!" She may have been defensive, but her natural curiosity made her want to know what he thought of her.

To her irritation, Brian laughed, too haughtily for her likes.

"What's so funny?" she demanded.

"You have a way with words," he declared, still grinning.

"Let's get back to the subject. Why do you think I'm suspicious of men?"

"The way you dress."

His words had been simple and direct and had zeroed right in on her white linen tailored suit.

Diane leaned back in her chair and wondered whether she really wanted to hear any of this. Her stomach tightened and she knew a part of her didn't, but another part couldn't resist finding out what this man thought of her.

"What's wrong with the way I dress?" she asked. Trying to appear calm, she casually picked up her wine glass and took another sip of the excellent Rhine wine.

"You're a beautiful woman with a beautiful body, but you hide it," he answered simply, then watched her intently, waiting for her reaction.

"How do you know I have a beautiful body?" she

challenged, then immediately wondered why she had asked such a thing.

"A man knows those things about a woman," he declared in an intimate tone.

"Like sixth sense?"

"Something like that."

"I see."

"I don't think you do."

There was something about his eyes as he stared at her, something so beautiful that Diane smiled.

"A penny for your thoughts," he said.

"I was wondering what time it was."

It was a half-truth. She was actually wondering if she should invite him home with her.

"Would you like to go?" he asked as she looked at her watch.

"In a little bit," she said softly, gazing into his warm eyes.

"Good."

"Good?"

"Yes, I like being with you, Diane. I'd like this night to go on forever."

"Thank you, Brian. I'm enjoying myself, too. And I do have to admit there may be something to what you said about men. It's not that I'm suspicious of them; it's just that I'm not used to being with them."

"What a waste."

"A waste or not, it's the truth."

"I'd like to get to know you, Diane. Are you involved with anyone now?"

"No," she replied simply, feeling very comfortable with this man and thinking that she was lucky to have met him.

He stared at her as if he doubted her words.

"Do you find that hard to believe?" she asked, wishing to know what he was thinking.

"Yes, as a matter of fact, I do."

"Why?"

"I would think it would be obvious to any man who saw you how lovely you are," he said, his eyes intense and mysterious.

Diane's lips automatically puckered in a frown upon hearing his words.

"You don't believe me, do you?" he asked.

"I didn't say that," she said defensively.

"No, but your lips did," he returned confidently.

"My lips," Diane repeated coyly, annoyed that he had so easily picked up on one of her habits.

"Yes, they have a way of giving your thoughts away," he told her with a devilish glint in his eyes.

Diane couldn't help but smile. She wasn't going to touch that remark with a ten-foot pole. She knew when to leave well enough alone.

"So, now that I've told you that I can't understand why some man hasn't dragged you off, I want you to know that I'm not involved with anyone either."

"Then I could ask you, too, why—"

"Why I'm not?" he asked with a laugh.

"Yes, precisely, a good-looking guy like yourself, not attached," she declared smugly, feeling more in control.

"I like that word, 'precisely.' To let people know what you want, you have to be precise."

"Sounds like your lawyer's mind talking."

"You're right about that," he said, smiling.

Diane suddenly noticed a very handsome couple,

walking arm in arm, obviously very much in love. Her eyes followed them as they passed by, and she breathed deeply, feeling more contented than she had in a long time.

"It must be the company," she heard Brian say, and she turned and looked up into his face with puzzlement in her eyes.

"You were drifting," he explained.

Diane laughed. "I was *thinking,*" she corrected him.

"What about?"

Diane stared at his brown eyes, wishing to fathom their mystery, and noted how truly sincere they appeared.

"I was just thinking how happy I am. I feel that we could be anywhere. Transported to a tropical island or something. That probably sounds silly, but it's the way I feel. It's been a perfect evening."

"Where would you like to be, Diane?"

"I don't know. I think right where I am."

"Thank you," he said, reaching out and catching her hand in his.

Diane's first reaction was to pull away. She didn't feel ready to accept this intimate gesture. But his hand was soft, warm, and comforting, and knowing she had nothing to fear, she left her hand in his care.

He seemed to sense her momentary uncertainty as he gently squeezed her hand as if to say that he was okay, he was safe.

Diane smiled, but she felt strangely awkward. The moment was too real and she was being affected too strongly. Anxiously she looked around and took in the now-empty tables and chairs.

"I think we've closed the place," she said with a

lightness she didn't feel, and kept her eyes on an impatient waiter, hovering around the entrance of the restaurant, waiting to go home.

"What do you say we get out of this joint?" Brian asked, his fingers gently kneading the back of her hand.

"I agree," she said, deciding she did want to invite him back to her apartment after all.

But the moment he released her hand and signaled the waiter, Diane began to question her decision. She wanted to be alone with him, yet she was aware of what the consequences could be. A woman simply didn't ask a man into her home on the first date without giving him the green light to make a pass.

Diane watched Brian carefully as he signed the credit card receipt. He was left-handed, and there was something elegant about his hands that excited Diane. She knew it sounded ridiculous to find a man's hands elegant, but his hand, though strong, had long, tapering fingers.

When he noticed her looking at him, he smiled. "What's going on in that head of yours?" he asked.

"Sometimes even I'm not certain," she answered evasively. "Ready?" she asked, and quickly stood.

Once out onto the sidewalk, Brian took her hand. Diane welcomed his touch and enjoyed walking down the street with him. She couldn't help but notice how people stared at them with almost a kind of envy in their eyes. Diane felt good to be on the other side of the fence for once.

As they walked, a light rain began to fall, and they quickened their steps. They were close to her apartment, and nearly reached the entrance of her building before a heavy downpour caught them.

They were both soaked by the time they entered the lobby. Instantly Diane knew she didn't have the heart to send him back out into the rain to get drenched. So, all her fretting about whether or not to invite him into her home was all for nothing. The decision had been taken out of her hands by an act of God, she thought with amusement.

"How would you like to come up and dry off?" she asked, not able to hide the smile that was dying to be born.

"Best offer I've had all day," he answered with a chuckle.

Well, that was easy enough, Diane thought as they walked to the elevators. But as they approached her floor, Diane found the silence unbearable and thought that even Brian could hear the loud pounding of her heart. What was all this nervousness about? she wondered. She was only inviting him in to dry off, *wasn't* she?

When they reached her door her hand began to tremble slightly, and she had a hard time unlocking the dead bolt.

"Let me," Brian suggested, and before she could protest, he took charge, taking the keys out of her hand and quickly opening the door.

"Thanks," she said, a frown on her face as she walked into her apartment, Brian following behind her. "Make yourself at home," she told him, and quickly turned on her heel, leaving him alone in the room.

Diane walked into the bathroom to check her appearance in the mirror. She was pleased to see the rain hadn't caused as much damage as she'd feared. Her hairdo was still intact, so no major repairs were needed. But her makeup was slightly smeared, and she grabbed a towel, patted her face dry, wiped away the streaks under her eyes, and retouched her eye shadow, blusher, and lipstick. Her suit jacket was pretty wet, and she removed it. Luckily, the white short-sleeved blouse beneath was dry. She took a clean towel out of the closet for Brian and returned to the living room.

Diane found him leaning against the mantel of her brick fireplace, his tall, handsome physique filling her world. Diane couldn't help but feel how right he looked standing there.

When his dark, friendly eyes met hers, she tossed him the towel.

"Thanks," he murmured, catching the offering. "That was one hell of a downpour," he added as he began drying off his face.

"You took the words right out of my mouth. How about some brandy to warm you up?"

"I'm fine. The rain actually felt good. It cooled me off," he declared, and smiled suggestively.

Diane stared at him, her face a stony mask. She was determined not to give him any encouragement.

"Do you mind if I take my jacket off?" he asked, a little too politely.

"No, not at all," she replied casually. "Let me help you," she offered sweetly.

Helping him off with his jacket, she hung it on the back of the chair next to them. She watched as he began to towel dry his hair. A drop of rain dangled from one curl hanging over his forehead and threatened to roll down his handsome face.

Without thinking she reached up, took the towel out of his hand, and wiped the water away.

He grasped her wrist, and she looked into his face.

"Take off your shoes," he ordered.

"What?" she asked, not believing her ears.

Brian chuckled softly. "Don't worry, I promised I'd be honorable, and I always keep my word. I only wanted to dry your feet. With those flimsy sling-backs on, they must be soaked. You could get sick," he stated almost paternally.

Diane grinned. The joke was on her. Here she thought the big guy was lusting after her body, and he was only concerned about her health.

"Well?" he asked, glancing down at her feet.

But have the man dry her feet—that was another thing!

"Oh, that's all right, really," she insisted, shifting her weight under his critical glare, not wanting him to know the idea made her uncomfortable.

"Come on, off with those shoes," he urged gently.

She stared into his dark eyes. Her feet were cold, and maybe she could handle feeling a little awkward. He was being so incredibly kind that she didn't have the heart to refuse him.

She smiled and he took the towel out of her hand. Without a word, she sat down on the sofa and raised her feet.

"Life is full of new experiences," she said with a nervous laugh as he removed her shoes.

With a sensitivity and tenderness she didn't know he possessed, he gently dried her feet. As he held the towel around her feet to make them warm Diane couldn't help wondering what it would be like to make love to Brian. If he took so much care with her feet, what would he do with the rest of her body? she mused.

Brian looked up. "How's that?" he asked, giving her toes a little squeeze.

"My feet will never be the same," she declared affectionately.

Their eyes met and held. Diane didn't know what had come over her, but for the first time in her life, she just wanted to be swept away by her emotions, without checking herself or weighing whether she was doing the right thing. She wanted to be in his strong arms, to feel the excitement of his body against hers. He thrilled her too much, just being close to him, not to want to make love to him.

Brian moved onto the couch with her. He cupped her chin in his hand, tilting her head back, ever so gently, raising her lips to meet his. Diane closed her eyes as his soft, warm lips caressed hers. It was the gentlest kiss she'd ever experienced, and she wanted it to go on forever, but suddenly, without warning, Diane was jolted back to reality. He was a stranger and they were alone together in her apartment. She knew where this kiss could lead if she wasn't careful, and she didn't know if she was ready to accept the consequences.

"No!" she exclaimed as she abruptly broke away from him.

Brian was looking at her intently, his cheeks flushed and his lips parted. "I'm sorry . . . I shouldn't have done that. I was out of line," he said, and quickly stood.

Diane automatically straightened up, then rose to her feet, facing him.

"I guess I should be going," he continued.

"It wasn't really all your fault. I did want to kiss you. I even hoped you would, but then I had second thoughts," she admitted.

"I'd never want you to do anything you didn't want to do, Diane," he said softly.

His words were exactly what she had wanted to hear, and they gave her the reassurance she needed. He was kind, incredibly attractive, and he wanted her, yet it seemed he wouldn't pressure her about sex. Diane realized she had nothing to fear from this man. Her desire to be with him was all that mattered now.

"Make love to me, please," she whispered, her heart beating so loudly she could hardly hear her own voice.

"Are you sure?" he asked tenderly. "I don't want to force you into anything."

Didn't he know how much she wanted him? she wondered, knowing that her desire was written on her face.

In answer to her unspoken plea and without a word, he lifted her effortlessly into his arms.

He whispered, his breath warm against her cheek, "You'll have to show me the way."

"It's through the corridor and off to the left," she somehow managed in a trembling voice, then wrapped her arms around his neck, allowing herself to be carried off, freely going on a wonderful journey.

Brian lowered her carefully onto the bed and then straightened. His sexual magnetism stirred her nerve endings. A peculiar expression crossed his face as his eyes probed to her very soul. It was her moment of truth, a moment when all guises fell away and only raw desire burned. She wanted him—never in her life had she ever wanted anyone as badly. A driving frenzy to be a part of him coursed through her body, a feeling so strong that it went beyond all rhyme or reason.

Anxious to make love, Diane began to undress. She unbuttoned her blouse, then raised her hips and unzipped her skirt. Slipping out of it, she proceeded to remove her undergarments, all the while her eyes riveted upon his face.

His glance slid from her face and roamed over her body. His mouth softened in approval. He lowered himself down alongside her and gently cupped her breast in his large hand. His gaze traveled back to her face and searched her eyes for a sign of objection. Her eyes told him what he wanted to know. He smiled softly, just before his mouth claimed her breast possessively, his tongue teasing her taut nipple. Her whole body responded with little tremors of delight. Releasing her breast, he looked at her. His eyes were like a smoldering flame, and a light blush brightened his cheeks. Diane's heart was joyous as she felt Brian's passion matching her own.

She smiled, reached out, and tenderly stroked his soft, curly hair, urging him close to her.

"Please, take down your hair," he said in a husky voice.

Diane automatically obeyed and began to remove the pins from her hair. Brian helped her, and when the task was completed he ran his fingers through her rich, gleaming auburn hair, which tumbled over her shoulders.

"You're beautiful," he moaned as his lips captured hers.

His mouth was wet, his kiss warm and filled with need, as his tongue boldly parted her lips and probed shamelessly.

His passion consumed her, and she kissed him with all her heart until she was sure it would surely break.

Finally, no longer able to control her desire for him, she broke away and cried, "I want to feel you close to me . . . I want your body next to mine!"

Quickly he removed his clothing and lay down beside her. His lips were anxious yet gentle as they explored every inch of her body. His tongue taunted her body until Diane could no longer hold herself back. She wanted him inside her. She wanted him to belong to her if only for a brief, few beautiful moments.

Her nails dug into the flesh of his back, urging him on top of her, wanting him to ride along with her. He responded and raised himself over her. He looked down at her, a look of innocence and vulnerability on his face. Could this rugged, worldly man be experiencing the same kind of desire that she was? Could it be possible that another human being could be filled with as much longing and desire as she was at this very moment?

She pulled him to her and wrapped her arms tightly around him. With one expert thrust he entered her, touching the very essence of her being. Something deep inside her snapped and came to life as her body moved with a frenzy and drive that she had never known was possible. Their bodies moved in unison, each driving the other on, building to an unbelievable height of passion. It was magic, it was mystical, it was just like she always thought it would be with someone she loved. It was as if the world had stopped on its axis. Nothing else mattered but Brian, she thought as all her inhibitions melted away. They had become so much a part of each other that she didn't know where she ended and he began.

Finally exhausted, their glistening bodies stilled. Brian carefully lowered himself to her side. He took her in his arms, and contented and protected, Diane closed her eyes and instantly fell into a deep, peaceful sleep.

The moment Diane awoke, she felt a tightness in her chest. She rolled slowly onto her back, careful not to wake Brian, his arm resting around her waist. She hoped that in her new position she'd no longer feel the sensation. But to her disappointment, it was still there, a nagging premonition that she had made a mistake.

She glanced over at the clock. It took her eyes a few minutes to focus in the dimly lighted room before she saw that it was only eight o'clock. Her body was still tired from their lovemaking from the night before, but her mind was like a live wire and Diane was suddenly aware of how troubled she really was.

She closed her eyes and snuggled closer to Brian. As she touched him he automatically reached out for her, wrapping her in his strong arms. She was momentarily comforted, but even with his nearness, she acutely felt their separateness. Being with Brian, experiencing him, was more than she had bargained for. But now it was another day, their lovemaking was over, and he was breathing deeply, sleeping soundly, and she was wide-awake.

It wasn't that she regretted her evening with Brian, but she wished that she had taken things a little slower. Where could they go from here? She couldn't bear to think that something so beautiful might only amount to a one-night stand. But she should have thought of that before she let her emotions get the better of her, she told herself. Brian didn't know her very well, so there wasn't any conceivable way for him to know how much being with him had meant to her. Nor did he know that this was a first for her. That never in her life had she ever given herself so completely to another human being.

As her glance darted over toward the window, bright light filtered through the cracks in the shade, promising another hot, brutal day. It would be like so many others. The continuity, the sameness, would prevail. But Diane seriously wondered if she would ever be the same again after being so totally touched by another human being.

Brian moved and suddenly awoke. He rolled over and kissed her lightly on the forehead.

"What's that for?" she asked with forced cheerfulness.

"For last night," he said warmly.

"Oh, my reward," she teased, then wished she hadn't.

Her words reminded her of that old saying about how a lot of truth was said in jest, and Diane was painfully aware that her words had actually been a plea for much-needed reassurance.

Brian stared at her, his dark eyes enigmatic, and

Diane regretted that she hadn't learned to mask her feelings better. She felt too vulnerable for a confrontation of any sort.

His lips parted as if he were about to say something, and Diane steeled herself, expecting the worst. But instead, Brian drew her close to him, his hands tight on her shoulders. He kissed her longingly, and for a moment, she forgot all her fears and gave in to his touch.

But once his kiss had ended, all of her confusion flooded back and she felt as if they were once again strangers.

"How about going to breakfast?" he inquired eagerly.

"You want to do that?" she asked, not overly enthusiastic.

"You have other plans?"

"Oh, no," Diane replied with a small laugh. "I'm just surprised."

He looked at her oddly but said nothing.

Diane knew she had to put distance between them, to figure out her feelings. It was all too easy to sink back into the false security of his arms. She could tell he wanted to make love to her again, but she pretended not to notice. She got out of bed and silently went about getting ready.

As they passed through the lobby, Diane had the urge to check her mail. Without a word to Brian, she walked over to her mailbox and removed the contents. She flipped through the mail. Suddenly her glance fell upon her name and address written in that same handwriting and on that same faded stationery. Another anonymous letter. She tensed. It *had* to be from the

61

same sender. Impulsively she ripped open the envelope and pulled out a folded piece of paper. In her haste, something fell out and dropped to the floor.

Quickly she bent over to see what it was, almost colliding with Brian, who had bent down to retrieve it for her. To her surprise she discovered that the envelope had been filled with newspaper clippings. She immediately scooped all but one of them up. Turning toward the stray clipping, she noticed that it was the article mentioning Wilding and Brian's law firm.

To her chagrin, Brian was picking it up. Without thinking, she grabbed it from him. Diane instantly regretted her action. She didn't know why she had acted that way—it was so unlike her. By the darkened look on Brian's face, she realized he hadn't liked it very much. "I'm sorry," she offered quickly with a nervous laugh, and shoved the letter into her pant's pocket.

"That's all right," Brian said.

But it wasn't. There had been no warmth to his voice, no understanding.

Without further comment they walked to an Irish pub nearby.

Diane tried very hard to be pleasant, but her conversation was forced and she felt uncomfortable. Her behavior was too obvious for Brian not to notice that something was wrong. But he didn't question her about it, and she was thankful.

How could she explain what she had done? Even she didn't understand why she had reacted so strongly to the clippings, especially the one concerning Wilding's use of Brian's law firm. Perhaps she was just feeling confused and vulnerable and the anonymous letter had only added to her insecurity. And yet, Diane thought, because the article made a reference to Brian, it was as though she were being protective of him. But it was all too much to comprehend, and she sighed.

Brian must have interpreted her sigh as one of boredom because he began to look for a waiter.

She studied Brian's profile and wished she could talk to him, explain her feelings. But she couldn't. In fact, she was once again questioning her own motives for sleeping with him on their first date. Why had she allowed her impetuous desire to throw her into a situation that was way over her head?

She wondered if he thought as badly of her as she thought he did. Diane also wondered if he would call her again. She doubted that he would, and she couldn't blame him.

CHAPTER FOUR

Brian caught the waiter's eye. He signaled for the check. The young redhead saw him and nodded. As the waiter sped away, Brian wondered whether he would see Diane again. He doubted it. Her behavior hadn't been very encouraging.

Throughout breakfast, Brian had remained outwardly calm, the epitome of a man in control. He had smiled at all the right moments, and he had even managed to make idle conversation. But his emotions had been anything but tranquil.

From the moment he had awakened, Brian had been aware that something was troubling Diane. His first reaction had been that she had been uncomfortable with—and maybe even regretted—their lovemaking. He had understood that, especially since neither one of them had been prepared for the intensity of their feelings. "Mornings after" could be pretty rough, but since they had explored each other's bodies so completely and freely as strangers, it was understandable that she might feel some awkwardness. He had wanted to reassure her by deliberately staying with her and showing her how much he wanted to be with her. He had asked her to breakfast to talk to her, to tell her how much he had enjoyed being with her and what she meant to him.

Making love to Diane had made him understand what it was like to make love with a woman he truly cared for. They had been perfect together, as if each had been intended for the other from the beginning of time. It was true his initial reaction had been purely physical, but being with her had made him realize how foolish he had been to think that one night could be enough. The mystery of her had enveloped him, and the memory of her beautiful, responsive body had embedded itself in his mind. For the first time in his life, Brian wanted to pour his heart and soul out to a woman to find out if they could have a future together.

But the words he had wanted to say to her had remained unsaid, he admitted to himself as he watched the tall waiter add up his check. Her change of mood had made him feel unsure of himself, made him feel that he had been wrong about her.

Turning back to Diane, he searched her face, trying to find something that would give him the truth. She smiled at him and he automatically smiled back. Could this beautiful creature, who behaved so politely and even, at times, a little shyly have been after only a fling? This thought bothered him so much that he couldn't bring himself to ask her the reason for her hot and cold treatment, afraid that his ego couldn't take a rebuff from her. At least he was being honest with himself, he thought as he finished his coffee. He knew that her eyes were upon him, but he didn't really want to talk. So he ignored her as he stared down into his empty cup.

The way she had snatched that clipping out of his

hand bothered him, too. It was as if she had something to hide. A boyfriend perhaps? He hated to think she might have lied to him about not being involved with anyone. But it wouldn't take much to make a woman like Diane feel guilty about being unfaithful, especially if she had received a letter from her boyfriend the morning after. So Diane's unexpected correspondence must have nailed the coffin shut.

"Thank you," the waiter said suddenly, placing the check in front of Brian and breaking into his thoughts.

Raising his head, Brian replied, "Thank you," then picked up the check.

As he glanced over the bill, he knew he would feel better if he could get his suspicions off his chest. But how could he broach the subject? He couldn't trust himself to be understanding. Before he had even taken the second bite of his eggs Benedict, a fury had overcome him. He had known if he'd said anything then, it would have been more like putting Diane on the spot and grilling her than asking a simple question. And that was not his style. He wouldn't allow himself to treat her that way. His ego was at stake too. He hadn't wanted her to know how much she had upset him.

As he signed the check, he knew he also had to take a look at his own feelings. Never before had he ever allowed a woman to get under his skin this way, and he didn't know what to do about it. Why should he be so angry if she did have a boyfriend? He had only just met her, and he had a lot of women friends himself. It was partially an issue of honesty. She had possibly lied about not having a boyfriend, but there was much more to it than that.

The bottom line here was that he hadn't talked to

her because he didn't want to betray his own feelings. Somehow it was hard for him to accept the fact that perhaps it was only sexual attraction that had made her respond to him. Had she used him as a sexual object only to be discarded like an old shoe?

His eyes narrowed as he stared at her. Those eyes of hers, those beautiful eyes—he should have listened to what they were saying instead of what he wanted to believe they said.

It was a bit too late for that, he thought.

"Ready?" he asked abruptly.

She gave him a startled look but replied politely, "Yes . . . And thank you. It was really nice."

He stared at her a moment longer, wondering what the truth was and if he would ever have the opportunity to find out. There was something troubling her, yet she hadn't made any move to let him know what it was. She certainly was a puzzle.

Without further conversation, he stood and she followed.

Diane sat in her apartment, not feeling very good about how she had left Brian. She was numb and confused. He couldn't be faulted for anything. He had been very polite and had even put up with her distant mood. But Diane couldn't help but wonder why he hadn't at least asked her if there was something troubling her. Was his politeness really a good sign? Instead of her interpreting his kindness as sensitivity to her mood, perhaps she should have read it as indifference.

Diane frowned. She glanced at her phone and wondered if she should call him to apologize for her behavior and try to explain. But what could she tell him? That being with him had totally disrupted her entire sense of herself? That never in her life had she experienced such desire and abandon and it scared her? No, she couldn't tell him anything like that. He would probably not believe her, and if he did, he would think her ridiculous. How could she expect him to understand that a woman of her age had never before been so moved?

What bothered her more than anything else was that the man who held the strings was someone she hardly knew. Her response to him had to have been a purely sexual one. It wasn't as if her feelings had resulted from spending time with him, from getting to know him and discovering that they shared a lot of beliefs and interests. What if she got to know him and found she didn't like him? Or couldn't agree with some of his ideas? Would she be so held by her physical response to him that it would be difficult to walk away?

All of this was very disturbing to Diane. It seemed as if she were at risk of having her whole life affected by Brian Scott. The strong walls she'd built around herself, which had so successfully protected her from loss, hurt, and pain, seemed to be crumbling.

Diane sighed deeply. She didn't have any answers, and she didn't know what to do with herself. She glanced at the clock. It was still early, only five o'clock. She thought of the clippings and her glance darted over to the white envelope on the coffee table in front of her. She wondered whether to look at them again, then decided it wouldn't help. She had looked at the clippings enough to know that she hadn't the foggiest idea what they meant.

Three of the clippings were copies of Diane's obituary column, and the other was the article about Wilding and Brian's law firm. What connection did they have with each other? It was odd that the same article about her neighbor that had caught her eye the other day would also be included. It was almost as if someone were spying on her. That thought gave her the creeps. But she forced herself to believe it was only a coincidence. The only one she had told about reading the article was Brian. He couldn't be involved in any way, she reasoned.

But *who* could be sending these letters and *why?* They in themselves didn't seem threatening, but then again, their purpose was still unknown. And not until it was would she really know whether there was any real danger.

Yet it disturbed her a great deal that not only did the sender know where she lived, but he—or she—also knew where she worked. Sending the clippings was a clear indication of that. What was even more alarming was that the second letter indicated that the first hadn't been just a fluke. Whoever had sent them had done so for a reason.

Finally, no longer wanting to dwell on something that couldn't be understood, Diane came to her feet and looked out her window. It was still light out and she decided she needed some therapy—a long walk. Exercise had a way of lifting her spirits. Besides, the fresh air would pick her up. Maybe she would take a stroll toward the East River, sit down on a bench, and watch boats go by. With this thought in mind, Diane felt a lot better.

She brushed her hair, braided it, and applied a touch

of makeup. Studying her face in the mirror, she firmly decided that the first thing she should do Monday morning was to get rid of her old-fashioned hairdo. Maybe she'd try a new hairstylist and get it cut shoulder length.

Grabbing her keys off the table, she rushed out the door toward the elevator. Moments later she was hurrying across the lobby's shiny marble floor. Running out of her building, she almost collided with Wilding. She started to apologize, but he seemed hardly to notice that she almost bumped into him. He was too taken with the very young and very attractive woman he was with.

Diane stopped in her tracks and turned to watch the couple. Wilding was certainly appealing enough—tall, thin, eloquently dressed, with silver gray hair. He slipped his arm around the brunet's slim waist and then whispered something in her ear as he guided her toward the entrance. The woman let out a high-pitched giggle, and it didn't take much to interpret the intention of his remark. Diane smiled to herself as she swung back around. That old fox! Boys will be boys, she thought, regardless of their age.

The article suddenly came to mind, and she wondered why anyone on earth would want to send her a clipping about this elegant older man. Diane shrugged. None of it made any sense to her at all.

Diane got through the rest of the day rather easily. She managed to put Brian and the mysterious letters into perspective, feeling there wasn't much she could do about either one.

She hoped Brian would call her again, but if he

didn't she knew she wouldn't call him. There was too much at stake for her to pursue him. She felt too vulnerable, and it was important to her that he should make the next move. She needed to know that his interest in her went beyond a mere physical attraction.

On the other hand, she would just have to wait to see if another letter were to follow. If it did, and it seemed threatening, she might have to take it to the police and discuss it with them.

With this all resolved, Diane felt more at peace, and when it was finally time to go to bed she curled up with a book, deciding to read until she got sleepy.

The phone rang, startling Diane out of a deep sleep. She wondered who could be calling at such an ungodly hour on a Sunday morning. After her restless night, it seemed like she had only just closed her eyes. Perhaps it was a wrong number. No such luck. The phone rang again. Her first impulse was not to answer it, but the caller was persistent. With much effort, she rolled over and waited a few seconds until her eyes focused on her digital clock next to her bed. It was eleven o'clock, much later than she had thought.

The phone rang again, and with much irritation, Diane grabbed the receiver off its hook.

"Hello," she said, trying not to sound too groggy.

"Did I wake you?"

Immediately she recognized Brian's deep voice and her heart leapt.

Diane felt slightly embarrassed that he had caught her sleeping so late in the morning and replied as casually as she could, "Yes, as a matter of fact, you did."

71

"Out last night?" he inquired with a sudden edge to his voice.

His unexpected question at first floored her, then amused her, washing away her momentary discomfort.

"No, but I couldn't sleep," she answered honestly.

"I wondered if you'd like to see a movie," he said, as if disregarding her words.

He had been given an opening to ask her why she couldn't sleep, and he hadn't even acknowledged what she'd said. It seemed she'd been right: Brian didn't want to get involved. This saddened Diane, and she questioned whether she should even bother to go out with him again.

"Diane, are you still there?" Brian asked.

"Sorry, I was just thinking," she replied simply, not feeling she'd owed him more of an explanation.

"Have other plans?"

"No, it's not that. It's just . . ." Diane broke her sentence off in midair, not knowing what she wanted to say.

"Now I know what it's like to be considered a one-night stand," he declared gruffly.

Diane was so surprised by his words that she couldn't do anything but laugh.

"Ouch!"

"What happened?" Diane asked with concern.

"Ever hear about the fragile male ego?" he came back in a humorless voice.

"What female hasn't?" she inquired lightly.

"Mine's just been stomped on. If I didn't know better, I'd think you had your hobnailed boots on."

"Oh, Brian, I couldn't help laughing. That was a funny line. I can't believe you said that."

"Well, what's a guy supposed to think? We spent a lovely evening together, and now I call you up and ask you out and I get a stall job," Brian said dryly.

"First of all, I'm sorry for the hesitation. Second, I don't know how you could think that of me."

"The one-night stand part?"

"Yes," Diane replied. Then, finding his sense of humor refreshing, she burst out with another round of laughter.

"I suppose you wouldn't let me in on the joke," he declared with irritation.

She knew her laughter was getting to him, and Diane really couldn't blame him for being angry. She had to try to control herself. Twisting the telephone cord around her finger, she admitted, "It's just that it's hard for me to believe that you'd really think I was only out for your body. Being with you was wonderful."

To her surprise, the other end of the line was chillingly quiet. What was the silent treatment all about? she wondered. Could he really be serious about her using him as a sexual outlet?

"Brian?" she asked, slightly annoyed.

"How about that movie?" he abruptly returned.

"You're asking me to a movie—is that what you're doing?" she inquired with an edge to her voice.

"Yes, and I think we should talk."

There had been a somber tone to his voice, and she wondered what he wanted to talk about. Had she been wrong about him? Maybe there was more to Brian Scott than just a pretty face, she mused.

"What do you want to talk about?" she pressed.

"About yesterday. What do you say?"

"I say you've got yourself a date," Diane answered, feeling more optimistic.

"Shall I pick you up at six? Take a look at the paper and let me know what you want to see."

"Sounds good to me."

"See you then," Brian said.

"Bye."

There was a click and the line went dead. Diane smiled as she placed the receiver on its hook. She was glad Brian had called. Now she would have a chance to explain her feelings. Or at least she would try. Since he had made the first move, she could do that much.

Diane dropped her head back onto her pillow. Turning on her side, she curled her legs under her, thinking perhaps she would sleep a little longer. After last night's tossing and turning, she probably had bags under her eyes. She would, after all, be seeing Brian, and she wanted to look her best. A small smile turned up the corners of her lips as she pulled the pillow from under her head and hugged it to her chest. She closed her eyes as she recalled his handsome face. That was the last thing she remembered before she fell into a peaceful sleep.

A few hours later, Diane dragged her contented body out of bed. The day was overcast so she spent most of the afternoon indoors tidying up her apartment.

As it neared six, a shakiness came over her. She was filled with excitement, knowing she would be seeing him soon. She tore her closet apart as she hunted for something to wear, something revealing.

Suddenly her intercom buzzed, and Diane reached for her sweater.

Hearing his voice over the intercom, she said, "I'll be right down."

Quickly closing the door behind her, Diane rushed toward the elevators.

The moment she saw Brian, her heart seemed to beat faster. He stood smiling as he watched her exit the elevator. He was unbelievably handsome. The memory of his touch came back to haunt her and her whole body seemed to glow with warmth. A tingling sensation ran up her spine and her cheeks flushed. His effect upon her was incredible! She immediately felt lighter, younger, and more sexually alive.

Diane returned his smile. She walked directly over to him, hoping he wouldn't notice her shaking knees.

"You look lovely," he murmured the moment she reached him.

"Thank you," she said, pleased he had noticed her sundress.

His glance dropped from her face and roamed over her bare shoulders, then to the bodice of her dress. His eyes shone with approval as they took in her cleavage made visible by the low-cut neckline.

"A bit of a change, wouldn't you say," he stated more than asked.

"You're not complaining, are you?" she inquired in a saucy tone.

"Not me," he replied, a mischievous look in his eyes.

"I didn't think so," she said boldly.

They were silent as they stared into each other's eyes, exchanging looks of appreciation.

"Anything in particular you'd like to see?" he finally asked, breaking the magic moment.

"There are a couple," she answered, almost in a whisper, mesmerized by his long dark eyelashes.

"Why don't we pick up the newspaper and check the times?"

"Did you want to talk before or after the movie?" Diane inquired, determined that they should clear the air between them.

Brian thought a minute before replying, "It's up to you."

Diane smiled. His words comforted her. A half smile graced his lips as though he understood, and they automatically turned to leave. Brian took her hand in his.

They walked to a local newsstand on First Avenue and bought a paper. Then they stopped at a restaurant to have a drink and look over the movie table.

Once seated, Diane glanced over the paper and then handed it to Brian.

"I think we should talk now, if you don't mind. Most of the movies have already started," she explained.

Brian nodded his agreement and placed the newspaper on the table next to him before he spoke. "I almost didn't call you, Diane. I wanted to, but I didn't think you were interested."

Diane stared at him. She couldn't blame him for feeling that way. But she wasn't ready to explain her behavior yet; she needed more proof that there was a reason to tell him her inner thoughts.

"Why *did* you call me?" she asked simply.

"I guess I've got skin as tough as elephant hide," he answered in a cocky way.

Diane glared at him. That wasn't the answer she wanted to hear.

"I wanted to be with you, you idiot. Couldn't you tell how much being with you has meant to me?"

The passion in his voice and the soft, earnest look in his eyes melted her fears away.

"I'm sorry," was all she could manage.

"There was obviously something wrong. I didn't ask you about it because I didn't want to pry and because I felt you regretted being with me."

"It wasn't that . . ."

Suddenly a waiter appeared at their table and placed menus in front of them.

"Would you like a drink?" the waiter asked.

"A white wine spritzer," she immediately answered, hardly aware of the person standing alongside of her, still caught up in Brian's words.

"An extradry Wolfschmidt martini on the rocks with a twist," Brian said.

Surprised that he was ordering such a strong drink, Diane eyed him suspiciously. Could this conversation be as difficult for him as it was for her? she wondered.

A moment passed as they both followed the waiter's departure.

Then Brian spoke. "I'd like to know what it was—why you acted the way you did."

"It's difficult for me to explain. First, because I'm not certain what happened, and second, I don't know if you'd understand," she hedged.

"Try me," he offered kindly.

Diane looked into his eyes. There was nothing to fear there; only warmth and concern showed through.

"I hadn't expected to feel the way I did. I mean, the

77

depth of feelings—" Her words broke off as she stared down at her hands and quickly folded them on the table. Uncomfortably she looked over at him.

Brian looked at her steadily, expecting more of an explanation. But she gave him none.

"That's it?" he asked in a disbelieving voice.

"In a nut shell."

What more could she say? She had practically told him that he had an unbelievable power over her. Did she have to spell it out?

"I'd just like to put this all behind us," he told her earnestly.

Diane stared into his large dark eyes. His vulnerability touched her. Could it be possible that this good-looking man shared her feelings?

"I missed your blue eyes," he said tenderly.

He reached over and gently stroked her hand. His touch instantly brought back all the emotions stirred up by their lovemaking, and Diane's heart fluttered.

"I want to know you, to hear your laughter, to find out where we can go from here."

He paused, but Diane knew he wasn't waiting for her comment. He rested his hand on top of hers, and the sudden strain that appeared on his face made her sense that he was struggling to find the right words.

He raised his hand slightly as his fingertips gently massaged her fair skin, and a soft smile turned up the corners of his lips.

"We don't have to discuss the other day again if you don't want to, but it's important for me to know if you want to see me and are free to have a relationship with me."

"I want to see you and I'm free to have a relationship," she returned directly as she squeezed his hand to emphasize her words.

"Are you sure?"

Diane didn't understand why he seemed to doubt her. She had already told him she wasn't involved with anyone. She could only assume it was because she was preoccupied the last time they saw each other and because she really hadn't explained her behavior.

"Yes, I am," she said simply.

"Good."

"Sorry to keep you waiting," the waiter suddenly announced at their side, placing their drinks in front of them.

"That's okay. Time has a way of flying when you're with a beautiful lady," Brian returned amicably.

The waiter jumped right in and replied, "Some guys have all the luck."

Diane laughed as the young fellow strolled confidently away, apparently very pleased with his sharp comeback.

"You're blushing," Brian told her, then chuckled softly.

Diane immediately felt her warm cheeks. "I guess I am. You have that effect on me," she teased, realizing how happy she was sitting across from this unusual man.

Brian glanced over at the newspaper as he briskly stirred his martini and declared with humor in his voice, "I think I'm getting pretty morbid. In my spare time, I find myself flipping through the paper to the obituary column. Reading it somehow makes me feel closer to you."

Diane laughed. "I don't know whether to take that as a compliment or not."

"I know, it's weird," he admitted, nodding his head and grinning comically. "But that's just how smitten I am with you."

Diane's lips automatically puckered before she took a sip of her drink.

"You don't believe me, do you?" he questioned as he raised his drink to his mouth. "You think it's a line, don't you?"

The mixture of wine and soda seemed to catch in her throat upon hearing his question. Swallowing slowly, she thought her words over carefully. "You're absolutely right. That did cross my mind. I'm sorry, but this is all very new to me. We need to go a little more slowly," she admitted.

Setting his glass down on the table, Brian replied, "That's fair enough. Tell me something about yourself."

"What would you like to know?"

"How about your work? Do you enjoy it?"

"Yes, I do. I've been feeling a little bored, though, the last few weeks, but now I think it's just the warm weather. Summer has a tendency to make me feel restless."

"New York is very different from where you're from?"

"Yes, it is."

"I can see that a lot in you."

"What?" Diane asked with raised brows.

"The small-town way," he answered affectionately.

Diane laughed. "Just because I'm from the Midwest doesn't necessarily mean I'm from a small town."

"Why are you so defensive about yourself?"

"I'm not defensive," she snapped.

"See what I mean?" he asked with a knowing grin. Diane gave him a dirty look.

"I'm sorry," he said. "You don't like my prying, do you?"

This man had a way of irking her every time he pounced on some quirk in her personality. But then again, he could read her pretty well, and in a way, she found this refreshing. "I guess I am a little protective," she managed.

"A little!" he declared with a roar.

"Hey, don't rub it in! Give you an inch and you take a mile!"

"I'm sorry, Diane. I just feel I have to break through that shell of yours. That's why I feel compelled to mention certain things I've noticed about you. It's my way of trying to break through. I guess it's a little crude, but I have this overwhelming desire to know you, to be close to you."

"You do?" she almost whispered.

"Yes, I do," he answered as a peculiar look came into his eyes.

Diane stared at him, wishing she could read his mind.

"You don't think a hard-nosed lawyer like me could have those kinds of feelings," he stated, intently watching her reaction.

"It's just that you seem so self-assured, as if you've been around a bit."

Once the words were out of her mouth, she knew that she hadn't said what she really meant.

Brian laughed.

"Does that sound funny?" she asked immediately.

"You make me sound so used. And so what if I'm self-assured? What does that have to do with my feelings for you?"

"Nothing, I guess. I'm glad I met you, Brian," she said warmly as she sipped her drink.

"I'm glad I called."

"Me, too."

"Here's to getting to know you," he toasted, raising his glass in salute.

"Here's to getting to know you," Diane returned, raising her glass to meet his.

They simultaneously tasted their drinks and set their glasses down.

A silence suddenly fell over them, and Diane's fingertips slid up and down the stem of her cocktail glass, feeling the smooth contour. Her mind drifted back to the day they met in the lobby of her building. It seemed so long ago. She felt that she had known this man all her life, but it was only a few days. If it hadn't been for Brian's appointment with Wilding, she might never have met him. The next time she saw the dapper old man, she thought playfully, she would have to plant a kiss on his forehead.

But the instant she thought of Wilding, the clippings strangely came to mind, and it was as if a dark cloud moved across her sunny mood. This feeling came totally out of the blue, and Diane couldn't understand what it meant. Nor had she been able to figure out why she had so instinctively kept the mystery letters from Brian.

She caught Brian studying her. Obviously her change of mood had immediately registered upon him.

But before he could ask her a question, she thought it best to put him on the defensive and asked him one instead.

"How are you and Wilding getting along?" she inquired casually.

"Fine. I think he's a great human being. He's extremely bright. I have a lot of respect for him."

"Why?"

"I think it's admirable, a man with his social position so concerned about helping people."

"How do you mean?"

Brian cocked one brow. "What is this—twenty questions?"

Diane smiled mischievously. "What's the matter? Don't you like talking about yourself?" she asked, giving him a good jab.

His eyes sparkled. "I guess I deserved that. Now, getting back to your question," he said, then paused as he took a sip of his drink. "He gives much of his time to charities—professional advice as well as money."

"Sounds like a very nice man," she returned with surprise ringing through her voice.

"I know it's hard to believe. Looking at the man, he doesn't seem the type. There are so few people who are in the position to help the less fortunate that do."

"I know what you mean," Diane said, feeling very peaceful.

She liked Brian's concern for humanity and felt very close to him. She suddenly wanted to tell him about the letters. Maybe he would help her discover what the clippings meant, especially the one about Wilding. She hadn't told anyone about them yet, and his feedback might be helpful.

"What's on your mind?" he asked, pulling her out of her thoughts.

But the moment he spoke, she decided that it wasn't the time to get into a discussion about her mysterious letters. "Not much," she returned quickly.

"What's the 'much' part?" he asked with narrowed eyes.

"I'm happy I met you, Brian. Or I should say, I'm happy you picked me up," she stated with a little laugh in her voice.

"Thanks a lot. You would have to throw that in my face."

"Well, you did, didn't you?"

"Great! You probably think that's how I spend my afternoons—waiting outside elevators, trying to pick up lovely ladies."

Diane laughed.

"Oh, so you *do*."

"That was my first impression," she teased.

"That figures," he said, then frowned.

"What do you say we decide on that movie?"

"Trying to change the subject?"

"Under the circumstances, I think it's a good idea, don't you?" she asked playfully.

Without another word, he handed her the newspaper.

"Let's see," she murmured as she flipped through the pages to the movie section. "What's your preference—comedy, mystery, blood and guts, or a love story?"

"Well, blood and guts is what's going on here. I think a change would be nice. How about a comedy?"

Diane chuckled as she scanned the list of movies.

"I certainly make you laugh, don't I?" Brian asked, somewhat amused himself.

"Yes, you do. And take it as a compliment. It's been a long time since I've been so happy," Diane said sincerely.

"Thank you, Diane," Brian replied softly, and a brilliant smile lighted his face. "Now, how about that movie?"

"How about a Bogart film?"

"A perfect choice."

CHAPTER FIVE

Dressed in a seersucker suit, Diane walked briskly out of her apartment building. Monday looked like a promising day. The sky was a bright blue and a refreshing breeze blew the wisps of hair around her face.

As she turned the corner, and was about to leave the complex, Diane spotted an ambulance parked in front of one of the buildings. A paramedic was standing outside. Wondering what had happened, Diane approached the man.

"Hi," she said.

"Hello," the man returned.

"What's going on?"

"Someone died," he answered casually.

"Oh, no. I'm sorry to hear that."

"The call was a probable cardiac," the young stocky medic stated in a businesslike tone.

"What was the person's name? I might have known him."

"It was a woman. A Mrs. Ruth Klein."

"That's a shame," Diane said, shaking her head.

"Goes on everyday," he replied indifferently.

"Yes, but I live over there," she retorted, pointing to her building. "And the death is rather close to me today," she added, annoyed at the man's callousness.

"It's been close to you before, lady," the attendant informed her in a cocky way.

"What do you mean?" she demanded as the man glanced toward the entrance of the building.

Diane waited, but he ignored her as though he hadn't heard her question.

"I'm a reporter," she announced loudly, hoping her title would evoke a reply.

"I wonder what's keeping Sam," he said, openly annoyed, kicking an imaginary object on the sidewalk.

"What did you mean about it being close to me before?" she insisted, not being put off by his irritation.

"You said you were a reporter—then you should know. I've been in your neighborhood a few times. The old people here seem to be dropping like flies."

Diane stared at him in disbelief. That was not the answer she'd expected.

"They have?" she asked.

"They sure have. Now, if you'll excuse me, lady, I have to get back to work."

Before she could say another word, the young man turned and sauntered over to another paramedic who had just emerged from the apartment building.

Diane shrugged and hurried toward First Avenue. It bothered her that she hadn't noticed there had been an unusual number of deaths in her area. It was, after all, her job. And more important, the deaths had occurred in her neighborhood and she should have known about them. Picking up her step, she decided to go through her files the moment she reached her office to check the validity of the medic's words.

Once she entered her office, the stack of phone messages left over from Friday immediately caught her eye and she flipped through them. Setting aside the most important calls, she returned those first. Finishing that task, she turned toward her files, but just as she reached to open a drawer her phone rang. She turned back to her desk and took the call, taking down some pertinent information on a celebrity to update his file.

As the day passed, Diane was more involved with her work and felt more relaxed than she had in a long time. She had to give the new man in her life some credit. She felt more alive and freer and looked forward to spending a lot of time with Brian. She hoped he felt the same way. His words definitely led her to believe he did.

Pleased with the new excitement in her life, Diane even remembered to call one of her girlfriends who highly recommended a hairdresser at Christian's, a posh salon located in the very fashionable Trump Tower. So without hesitation, she phoned the salon to make an appointment. To her disappointment, the earliest available opening was the following Friday. She could hardly wait. Once Diane made up her mind to do something, she wanted to get it done.

The time flew and before Diane knew it, it was time to go home.

As she walked toward her apartment building, she couldn't help but notice the spring to her step. She smiled to herself. Life was good. Knowing Brian had made a difference. He had told her he cared about her and wanted to see her. She had spent a wonderful evening with Brian, and after the movie, he had not pushed sex, making her feel that he really did want to get to know her. She had not expected, nor had she been looking for, a special man in her life, but it had happened. The timing was perfect. Not only that, Brian was simply perfect.

Once inside her apartment, Diane dropped her bag and keys onto a chair and walked toward the air conditioner. The moment she reached to switch it on, she remembered that she'd forgotten to check her files about the deaths.

"Oh, darn!" she exclaimed, annoyed that she hadn't even given it a second thought.

Turning the air on, she stood for a moment while a cool breeze blew across her face. Now that she was home, she wondered if there was anything she could do to find out how many of the deceased were from her area.

A thought popped into her head, and she quickly walked over to her desk where she had placed the anonymous letters. Opening a drawer, she took out the white envelope and opened it. She scanned the names in the obituary columns to see if any of them sounded familiar. To her chagrin, they didn't. But then again, she didn't really know most of her neighbors by their names, only their faces. The only thing she could do was look up their names in the phone book, and if they were listed, she could find out where they lived. Feeling very smart, Diane moved, but then realized she didn't know where on earth she had put the telephone book. As organized as she appeared in her professional life, her true, rebellious nature had a way of rearing its ugly head when it came to her housework. Then it dawned on her—the bathroom! The last time she straightened out the bathroom closet, she'd hidden the telephone book on the bottom shelf.

She found that one of the deceased lived in the

Eighties on the East Side and another one was not listed. Feeling somewhat discouraged, she noted the third person's name on the list, a Mrs. Shirley Peters, and flipped through the telephone book. Her index finger slid down the long list of Peters until she found an S. Peters listed. To her surprise, the address given was that of the building across from hers. This discovery was like a shot of adrenalin, and Diane quickly checked all the remaining names. With the task completed, she discovered that on each clipping there was at least one person from her neighborhood complex.

Diane leaned back in her chair. Now that she had learned this much, she still didn't know what it could mean. She stared at the names. Then it hit her—the words from the letter! "You don't know what's going on in your own backyard" flashed through her mind, and Diane made the connection. Whoever had sent her the clippings was trying to tell Diane about the deaths in her neighborhood . . . But why? The person was obviously asking for help of some sort, but why had the clipping about Wilding been included? Was Wilding going to die? she wondered. Diane sighed wearily. None of it made sense to her, and the only thing she could do was wait and hope that the person would contact her again.

Suddenly she wished that she would hear from Brian. She glanced over at her phone and wondered if he would call. Then she decided to make herself something to eat and got up and went into the kitchen.

Around eleven, she got ready for bed, yawning as she undressed. Brian hadn't called, and she finally thought that maybe it was better he hadn't, after all. She had told him that she wanted to take their relationship slowly, and perhaps he was going to give her some breathing room. She needed the time to deal with the intensity of her feelings for him. They had a strong hold over her, and she wanted to be more in control so she wouldn't get in the way of herself.

Diane yawned again as she switched off the light and slipped under the covers.

Brian stood in Diane's lobby, flipping through the papers in his briefcase. He felt a little funny about being there, especially since the probability of running into her was extremely likely. He was concerned about being reproached by her. A few days had passed, and he had deliberately not called her. Not that he had regretted seeing her. As a matter of fact, he was glad that he hadn't allowed his pride to keep him from asking her out again. She had made him feel that they could have a future together, and that he had been wrong about her having a boyfriend. Yet he felt uneasy about pushing himself on her.

Brian found and pulled out the will that had been prepared for Wilding and looked it over to make certain everything was in order. Satisfied that it was, he slid the will back into his case, in front of the other papers, and snapped the case closed. Then he reached over and pressed the elevator button. His mind suddenly drifted back to the first time he had seen Diane, standing in front of her mailbox. It was incredible how much she had excited him then even though he hadn't even known her. Now that he did know her, he wanted her more than ever. But the power she held over him made him feel uneasy. For the first time in his life, he didn't feel in control.

He wanted to be with her—he knew that much. But he questioned the longevity of his feelings. Could his emotions for Diane be only passion? Would they fade with time? He hoped not, but he had to admit that a part of him wished it were true. Brian had recently done some soul-searching and really questioned whether he was ready to make a commitment. If he did, he knew it would be for life. He never did anything halfway.

The doors opened and Brian turned toward them. To his surprise, Diane walked out of the elevator, looking lovelier than ever. He found himself suddenly ashamed of his thoughts. She smiled at him so warmly, so innocently, that it made him feel even worse. She had no idea of his doubts. Under her bright, curious gaze, Brian automatically shifted his weight uncomfortably.

"Why, hello," Diane said, surprised and yet pleased to see Brian and thankful that she had taken extra time with her makeup.

"You caught me," Brian teased, but his joke fell flat.

Diane studied his face for a moment. There was something different about him, but she couldn't put her finger on what it was. But one thing was for certain: Diane was happier to see Brian than he was to see her.

"Are you visiting Wilding?" she inquired, not knowing what else to say.

"Yes," he answered, but offered no further explanation.

"Oh, and here I thought you were waiting for me," she joked.

Brian laughed, but his response sounded forced.

"Unfortunately I'm only here to deliver a will to Wilding," he said.

He seemed unhappy about something, she thought as a puzzled expression crossed her face.

"The testatrix had instructed me to turn over the original to Wilding upon her death," he explained, misinterpreting her confusion.

"The what?" Diane asked perplexedly.

Brian laughed. "Sorry, that's lawyers' jargon. *Testatrix* is the term used for the woman whose will it is."

"Oh, that explains everything," Diane declared lightly, and glanced down at her watch.

"Have an appointment?" he inquired, his voice warmer, making Diane feel her first impression about him might have been wrong.

"Yes, as a matter of fact, I do—an appointment with my desk," she said with a little laugh in her voice. "By the way, I hope you don't mind my asking, but who died?"

"A woman named Ruth Klein."

"Mrs. Klein," Diane repeated with surprise.

"Did you know her? She was from one of the buildings around here."

"No, but I saw the ambulance the other day. You're taking her will to Wilding? I don't understand."

It wasn't like her to be nosy, but the unexpected connection of the dead woman to Wilding piqued her curiosity.

"It's because he's the executor of her will," Brian answered.

Upon hearing his words, Diane felt a knot in the pit of her stomach. Not understanding her reaction and not wanting Brian to see her sudden shakiness, Diane quickly declared, "Oh, I see. Well, I'd better get going."

"Okay, I'll call you later. Maybe we can get a bite to eat," Brian suggested.

Diane smiled. "I hope you do," she returned pleasantly, then turned on her heel and walked briskly through the lobby.

But once Diane reached the sidewalk, the momentary calm that she had felt immediately vanished. It was as though her balloon had been pricked and deflated. A sudden heaviness came over her.

Upon reaching her office, Diane tried to throw herself into her work to dispel her nervousness. But no matter how much she tried, she couldn't concentrate. The fact that Wilding was the executor of the dead woman's will stirred up too many thoughts. Was it possible that Wilding had known some of the other people listed in the clippings? she wondered.

The words "Please look around and put an end to innocent people being preyed upon" came to mind. It wasn't possible that the renowned Wilding could somehow be involved—or was it? Just looking at the man, anyone would notice his wealth, breeding, and charm. It didn't seem possible that he would have any reason to do anything so underhanded.

Diane shook her head. Her imagination had to be running away with her.

"No, it couldn't be true," Diane muttered at precisely the exact moment that her boss poked his head into her office.

"Talking to yourself now," John declared with amusement ringing through his gruff voice.

Diane chuckled. "You caught me," she retorted

lightly, hoping he wouldn't notice her troubled state of mind.

"You know, that's one of the first signs of—"

"Cracking up?"

"I'm glad *you* said it," he returned affectionately.

"Yes, I know. That's why *I* said it."

No matter how much Diane tried, she couldn't get her recent discovery out of her head. She felt she had just been given one piece to the puzzle, but she didn't know how or where it fit.

"How about a strong cup of coffee for whatever ails you?" he asked.

Diane looked at her boss and noted the concern in his eyes. "I'm all right—really I am," she told him in the most reassuring voice she could manage.

John eyed her suspiciously. "Why don't you tell me what's wrong? You can't pull the wool over this old fox's eyes," he said kindly.

"I suppose there's no way of getting around it, is there?" she asked.

"No. After all, I'm the boss."

"And what the boss wants, Diane has to do," she supplied with a laugh.

There were times, like right now, when Diane wished that she hadn't allowed her relationship with John to become so personal. It was easy to understand how it had happened. He and his wife had welcomed her into their home on many occasions, especially to celebrate holidays when she couldn't go home, and John had taken an almost paternal interest in her from the first.

But as Diane looked into the kind old man's eyes, she knew that it was too late to think about that. They were friends, and it was very natural for him to be concerned. She wasn't very good at masking her feelings.

Obediently she stood and led the way to his office. She walked into the room and directly over to the chair in front of his desk. She sat and turned to face her boss. He closed his door. That was a sure sign that he wanted a serious conversation.

Diane sighed. He must mean business, she thought.

"How do you want your coffee?" he asked as he moved in front of the coffee machine.

"Black."

She usually liked her coffee with a lot of milk, but right now, she felt she needed something stronger.

"It's that bad?" he asked lightly before taking two cups down from the shelf above him.

"It's not that it's so bad . . . It's just that you'll probably think I'm crazy."

John handed Diane her coffee, then walked around his desk and sat in his leather chair, placing his coffee in front of him.

"I thought we already diagnosed your state of mind," he teased, a wicked glint in his eyes.

Diane laughed. "Boy, I can see I'm not going to get any sympathy around here!"

"No, you're right about that. Okay, so tell me. What's wrong?"

Diane smiled and lifted her coffee cup.

"Be careful. That's hot," he warned.

"I will," she answered, and slowly sipped her coffee. Setting the cup down, she asked, "What do you know about Stephen Wilding?"

John stared at her as if not believing her question.

"I told you that you'd think I was crazy."

"This has something to do with Wilding?" he asked in a surprised voice.

"Sort of."

Her boss folded his arms and leaned back in his chair. "I've heard his name a lot, but I don't know too many details about him," John admitted. "Tell me about him."

"He's been mentioned in the society columns as one of the most eligible bachelors around. He was married to the late Debra Jennings, of the Jennings steel mill fortune, and since her death, his name has been linked to many charities. How's that?"

"Sounds like you've done some digging," he said, but not with the enthusiasm she'd hoped for.

"Yes, I have, and he lives in my building," she offered.

"Oh, I see," he replied, but the lack of enthusiasm in his voice signaled that he didn't see anything.

"I guess I should get to the problem," she stated, realizing that her boss still didn't have the foggiest idea where this conversation was taking him.

He nodded in agreement and his eyes widened as he waited for her to explain.

"First of all, I've received two anonymous letters. The first one said—I have it memorized by heart—'You are bright at what you do, but you don't know what's going on in your own backyard.' Then a few days later I got another one. There was nothing written on it, only a folded piece of paper with four newspaper clippings. Three of the clippings were from my obit column, and the other one was about Wilding,"

Diane told him, then paused to take another sip of her coffee.

"Do you feel threatened, Diane? If you do, you can contact the police, and you should also get in touch with the post office. They have a special division that investigates problems like crank letters."

"No, I don't really feel threatened—that's the funny part. It's more like someone is asking for my help."

John swallowed some of his coffee. "Why do you say that? And what's the connection with Wilding?"

"Well, this is the crazy part," she began, and paused.

"Go ahead. You've stirred up my curiosity. You can't stop now."

"I can't help but feel that he's connected to this in some way."

"I still don't understand what you're saying," her boss told her, an edge of impatience to his voice.

"I don't know exactly, but there *is* a connection. Today I learned that he is the executor of Ruth Klein's will. When I left for work the other morning, I saw an ambulance parked in front of a building close to mine. I asked the medic what had happened and he told me that someone had died. I pressed him for more information and he told me that the person's name was Ruth Klein. I also found out that a few other people have died in my area just recently."

Diane had stopped, hoping her boss would come to the same conclusion she had.

"So, Wilding is the executor of this dead woman's will."

"Don't you see? The sender of the anonymous letter told me that I didn't know what was going on in my own backyard. Then I find out that several people have died in my neighborhood. I looked up the addresses of the people listed in the clippings, and I found that several of them lived in my area."

"That's some coincidence," he agreed, his voice even, devoid of emotion.

"Yes, that's what I thought," Diane said, glad that her boss had agreed. "Then when I found out that Wilding had known the dead woman, I couldn't believe it. Don't you think that's strange?"

"Diane," John began, then shook his head, "I hope you don't think that Wilding could be involved in anything underhanded."

"Well, I don't know what I think. I only know that the article about him was included and—"

"And you just might be trying to create a little suspense to offset the boredom you've been feeling," he reminded her.

"I know that I told you I was bored, but this has nothing to do with that. You told me to take Friday off, that maybe all I needed was a rest, and you were right. But I'm telling you there's something going on, and I have a feeling—a strong one—that Wilding is somehow involved."

"Wilding is a highly respected man."

"I know that. That's what I have a problem with, too. Every time I've seen him, he's appeared to be the epitome of wealth and good breeding. His name has been linked to half a dozen charities, and the ladies seem to find him quite charming." She sighed deeply.

"What about you?" her boss inquired with raised bushy brows.

"I have to admit he's a very attractive older man.

But you can't say I'm making up those letters," Diane insisted, trying to argue her flimsy case.

"No, I can't. It does seem odd. But, Diane, no one will believe you unless you have some kind of proof. Wilding is a very important guy, and you could be asking for trouble," he warned.

Diane sighed again. She knew he was right, even though she had hoped for more support. "I can't help but believe that the person who wrote those letters wants something from me—help or something. I just hope whoever it is comes forward and tells me what I can do," she said dispiritedly as she got to her feet.

"I didn't tell you what you wanted to hear, did I?" he asked in a kind voice.

"Not exactly, but I do know you care, and that's important to me. Maybe I always wanted to be Dick Tracy when I grew up, and now I'm coming of age," she mused, chuckling slightly.

"You do feel better though, don't you?"

"Yes, thank you, but I haven't said I was giving up," Diane told him stubbornly, shaking her index finger at him.

"I know you haven't," her boss declared with a laugh. "I've never known you to give up anything without a battle. If you have a hunch about something, you'll look under every rock to prove your case," he said affectionately.

"You know me all too well . . . I'm going to follow this up. And what if I do discover that Wilding's not at all what he's cracked up to be?"

"Just what do you have in mind?" John asked with amusement ringing through his voice.

"I see a story here and a great opportunity to prove

what a terrific reporter I can be. What do you say? If this pans out, would you let me write a feature story?"

John flashed her one of his noncommittal grins.

"What if I wrote a wonderful story—would that make a difference in finding me a new spot on the paper?" she pressed, determined to get an answer.

"We'll see," he answered. "That's all I can offer at the moment."

"Well, that's good enough. Now, I'd better get back to work," she said, her spirits higher.

"It's about time," he agreed loudly.

Turning back to him, she murmured, "Thank you," then quickly exited his office.

Diane was more determined than ever to find out what the anonymous letters meant. Back at her office, she glanced over the death announcement for Mrs. Ruth Klein. She was the wife of the late renowned neurologist Dr. Michael Klein. The death notice had been placed by her synagogue, and there had been no mention of children or any other surviving relatives. She wondered if it were possible that all the other decedents were members of the same synagogue and knew each other. Quickly she took the other clippings out of her purse and went over them. To her disappointment, there was no connection. Services for one had been held at a Catholic church, another was a member of a Protestant church, and as to the last one, no mention of religion was given.

"Darn!" Diane muttered.

She thought she was really getting somewhere, only to find out that she was still stuck in the mud. She threw the last clipping onto her desk, feeling very discouraged.

But then a thought came to mind: there was *another* connection! In addition to living in the same area, they had all been widows! Feeling rejuvenated, Diane grabbed the clippings to reconfirm her memory. She was right! And not only that, none of them had any children or other surviving relatives listed.

So, there was a pattern after all! Now, how was Stephen Wilding involved? she wondered. Perhaps he knew them all. He did seem to be quite the "ladies' man," and she could easily see how appealing an older woman would find him.

Just then her intercom buzzed, and Diane jumped. Quickly recovering, she pressed the button down. Her assistant announced that Brian Scott was on the line.

"Thank you," she said as a smile lighted up her face. Depressing her extension, she said, "Hello, Brian."

"Not interrupting you, am I?" he asked in a bright voice.

"I have a few minutes," she replied affectionately. "What can I do for you?"

"I wanted to know if you wanted to get some grub later?"

Diane laughed. "You've been watching too many westerns," she teased.

"And here I thought that was a new approach," he replied wittily.

"You don't need a new approach. The old one works perfectly well."

Brian chuckled, making Diane's heart sing.

"I'm taking that as a compliment."

"And that's precisely how it was meant," she said softly. "And about that 'grub'—I'll be ready at seven."

"I'll pick you up at your place. I'm looking forward to being with you," he murmured.

Diane held the phone next to her cheek a moment longer, the memory of his deep voice still ringing through her ears. He had said that he looked forward to being with her. Did that mean what she hoped it meant, that she would be in his arms later that night?

Just then her intercom buzzed, and she was informed that a prominent senator had just died and a request had been made for any information she might have on him. Obituaries and background material were often written about celebrities while they were still living, for future use, and Diane often got calls like this one. She promptly went to her files to see what current information she might have on him, before checking their library.

Diane glanced at her watch. It was later than she thought when she hurried into the entrance of her building. As she headed toward the elevators, she wondered if she had received any mail. She didn't want to be late for her date with Brian, but at the same time, she couldn't resist passing her mailbox without checking it for mail. Perhaps there would be another of the mysterious letters. Her curiosity won out as she turned to her left. Besides, it would only take a minute, she argued as she opened her purse and took out her keys. Quickly she unlocked her mailbox. It looked as though she had hit the jackpot. The box was stuffed. Pulling out advertisements and magazines, she found there were only a couple of letters.

Suddenly she felt as if a jolt of electricity shot through her. She had received another of the anonymous letters! Diane immediately ripped open the envelope. She pulled out a folded piece of paper, and inside was another clipping!

Diane stared at the clipping in disbelief. It was from yesterday's obituary column. It was exactly the same one that she had looked at today that had listed Mrs. Ruth Klein. But in this copy, Mrs. Klein's name had been underlined in red, and above her name, the word *Help* had been written.

A calm suddenly overcame her. It was the same kind of reaction she always had when the answer to an important problem dawned on her. The clipping had given her all the proof she needed to know that she had been on the right track. It made her believe that she had been right all along about the sender's concern for the people who had died in her area. And the word *Help* written on the clipping further confirmed her suspicions about the sender's intentions. He or she was definitely asking for *her* help. Then could her suspicions about Wilding also be right? she wondered. Everything pointed in that direction.

And he was Brian's client. What would Brian think about all this? Brian! Diane suddenly remembered her date and shut her mailbox. Turning, she quickly headed toward the elevators, only to run into the dapper Mr. Wilding! The doors had just opened, and he took off his hat. Mrs. Dempsey stepped out of the elevator, and Diane thought that Wilding nodded to her or said something. But the little white-haired woman sped by him without even acknowledging the man. Diane was about to say something to her, but the elderly woman appeared to be upset about something, and Diane didn't want to disturb her.

Suddenly Diane realized that she'd been staring at Wilding. As his gray eyes met hers, Diane felt embarrassed.

"Going up?" he asked politely.

"Yes, thank you," she returned sweetly, almost ashamed of her suspicions regarding the nice old man.

"Let me hold the doors for you," he offered gallantly, and placed his hand against the inside of the door.

Diane smiled her thanks and hurried toward the opened doors.

"Thank you," she murmured again as she walked into the car.

"It's my pleasure," he answered in a very dignified voice.

Luckily another woman joined them, one that Wilding seemed to know, and he turned his attention toward her. Diane couldn't help but study the man out of the corner of her eye.

He was tall and thin and looked very elegant in his khaki gabardine suit. He wore a white poplin shirt with a button-down collar and a silk rep tie. His shoes were expensive looking, and his silver hair was distinguished. He clearly looked like a man of the world.

The huge smile on his pretty friend's face showed that the woman found him very appealing. And Diane had to agree. Despite his age, the man radiated charm. If Wilding was a crook, he certainly didn't look the part.

Diane was finally on her floor and headed toward her apartment. She wished that she had waited to open her mailbox until after her date with Brian. That way, she might have avoided running the risk of ruining their time together as she had done the last time. She just *had* to forget about this latest discovery for the rest of the evening and enjoy herself with Brian. It wasn't fair to him for her to be preoccupied with the letters. She didn't want to make the same mistake twice. She was excited about seeing Brian and would be sure to center all her attention on him.

With the letter temporarily put out of mind, Diane's spirits rose. She unlocked her door and threw her purse onto the chair. And as the door slammed behind her she rushed toward her bedroom to get ready for an evening with her hunk.

His eyes were inviting, his mouth was sensual, and his smile was sunny as Brian sat across from Diane. He was wearing a beautifully tailored navy linen blazer with gold-toned buttons over a white button-placketed cotton shirt. His blond wavy hair was windblown. She thought he looked incredibly handsome.

It had only been a few days since she had been with him, but it seemed like an eternity. The restaurant he had chosen was a very romantic place with excellent food and prompt service, but all Diane could think about was how much she wanted to be alone with Brian! She wanted to feel his body once more next to hers, to throw herself into total abandonment and bliss. Nothing else mattered.

CHAPTER SIX

Brian glanced at his watch.

"What time is it?" she asked immediately.

"Eight thirty."

Too early to go home, she thought. How could she finagle being alone with Brian without appearing too eager?

"How about coming to my place . . . for a nightcap?" he asked suddenly.

Not only is he handsome, she thought, but he's also a mind reader.

"I thought you'd never ask," she replied, smiling. She felt a little self-conscious and quickly looked away from Brian and sipped some Chianti.

Brian lived within only a few blocks of Diane, but the decor of his apartment made their homes seem worlds apart. Hers was a traditional one-bedroom apartment, modestly decorated with antiques and modern furniture. His was a renovated loft—a stunning example of what money, good taste, and expert planning could achieve. The bleached parquet floors were covered by finely textured Oriental rugs. The walls were painted turquoise. A group of richly colored paintings hung on one wall, while a gorgeous

Flemish tapestry dominated the other. A large picture window gave a breathtaking view of the East River and the Queensborough Bridge. His apartment was both elegant and spare, and Diane immediately felt at home.

As they sat on his plush gray sofa he looked at her seriously. "I brought you here for a reason," he said finally.

He was too close to her. Her heart pounded in her chest, and the faint aroma of his limey after-shave filled her senses.

"I should have guessed you had an ulterior motive," she said offhandedly.

"Would you like something to drink?"

"No, thanks. I'm fine right now," she answered, and stared into his dark eyes, wondering what he was about to tell her.

A tense look came across his handsome face. "I have a confession to make," he began slowly.

She wanted to ask him what he meant, but something made her hesitate. She sensed that it was difficult for him to talk and didn't want her words to interrupt him.

He touched her chin and gently tilted her head up toward his. "I think I'm falling in love with you," he said, and a light blush came to his cheeks.

Her heart leapt. His words had been just what she had been longing to hear though she hadn't been able to admit it, even to herself.

But it had all happened so quickly, so unexpectedly, that Diane almost wanted to pinch herself to prove she wasn't only dreaming. She badly wanted to tell him how she felt about him but couldn't trust the tears that were welling up in her eyes. All she could do was offer him a smile.

Brian smiled softly in return and moved his arm around her shoulder, his fingertips resting on the back of her neck.

Diane's eyes closed as his lips claimed hers. A ripple of delight flowed through her body, and instinctively she wrapped her arms around his neck. He pulled her up against him. A moan rose in her throat and her breasts instantly surged at the mere contact with his strong, manly chest.

Releasing her lips, he looked intently at her, his eyes vulnerable.

"I've missed you," he said in a quiet voice that she'd never heard before.

"I've missed you, too," she whispered before their lips met again.

His kiss was so unbelievably seductive. A fierce passion took over her. She kissed him with the very essence of her soul. If she couldn't tell him how she felt about him, she could show him. Diane was swept off on a magical journey that she wished would never end.

Breaking free at last, Brian implored in a husky voice, "I want to make love to you . . . You're driving me crazy!"

"Darling, please!" Diane cried, feeling as though her body would explode from sheer need.

He gently eased her down onto the sofa. Leaving a burning trail along the path they traveled, his hands quickly and expertly unbuttoned her blouse. He opened the sheer fabric and stared down at her full bosom. The glow in his eyes told her all she needed to know, and a thrill circuited up her spine.

He lowered himself over her, and his mouth gently caressed one aroused nipple. Her body responded with little tremors of delight.

"I love you," he moaned as his warm mouth recaptured hers.

Diane hardly remembered moving to the bed or her clothing slipping away as she gave herself to this very special man. She reacted so completely to his touch that she knew she belonged to him and he to her. Making love to Brian was the most beautiful experience she had ever known. She thought the first time had been perfect, but this time was even better.

Finally, with their longing for each other satisfied, their glistening bodies lay still, their bodies entwined. The world had stopped, and as the minutes passed, their separateness became more apparent until Diane realized it was time to leave.

With great reluctance, Diane rose and began to dress.

"Hey, where are you going?" Brian asked in a sleepy voice.

"Home," she replied simply as she slipped into her skirt.

"I was hoping I could wake up with you in my arms," Brian said, his disappointment obvious.

"I know, but I do have to be at the office early, and I think it's best if I stayed in my own apartment . . ." she explained, her voice trailing off.

"If you're certain," Brian said, and he slowly sat up.

"I am, and please stay in bed. I can get home by myself," she insisted.

"I wouldn't think of letting you go home by yourself," he told her firmly as he got out of bed.

Silently they dressed, each seeming to be lost in thought. Diane felt a little guilty about her departure. She had not exactly told the whole truth. She knew she had hurt Brian by not staying, but things were moving too quickly for her. She was afraid that if she accepted his invitation to stay the night, she might begin to think that their lovemaking meant more than it really did. She didn't want to get too comfortable with him, too dependent on him. After all, they had only known each other for a short time, and she needed to cool her feelings toward him until she knew where she stood with him. Could she really believe he loved her? Could he know in such a short time? She had to put distance between them until she knew him a little better, before she allowed herself to get too involved with him.

Silently Brian walked her home.

As they approached her building, a small, short woman sped past them. Catching a glimpse of her troubled face, Diane immediately recognized Sarah Dempsey. Diane wondered what was wrong with her. It was the second time this past week that she had looked upset. Diane suddenly felt guilty for not talking to her the first time she had noticed her problem. They were casual friends, at least, and had always talked to each other whenever they met. Until recently the woman had always been happy. Diane couldn't imagine what could cause such a drastic change in her personality. Maybe she wasn't well, Diane thought.

"Where'd you go?" Brian asked, squeezing her hand.

"I was just thinking about the woman who just passed us," Diane said.

"You know her?"

"Yes. You probably don't remember, but she's the one who gave you a dirty look, coming out of the elevator."

"You mean the day I met you?"

"Yes."

"I should have known she was a friend of yours," he remarked dryly.

"Whatever that's supposed to mean," Diane shot back, though her thoughts were still on Mrs. Dempsey.

"She probably thought I was going to murder you in the elevator," he said, and chuckled.

But his humor was wasted. Diane couldn't dismiss Sarah from her thoughts. "Brian, I hope you don't mind, but I think something is wrong with her and I'd like to see if I can help. Would you excuse me for a moment?"

"Sure, I'll wait outside."

"Thanks," Diane replied over her shoulder as she hurried off, hoping to reach the woman before she got into the elevator.

"Mrs. Dempsey!" she called, trying to get her attention.

The old woman swung around and faced Diane. There was a startled look in her eyes, but she forced a smile.

"Please wait," Diane said as she hurried toward her.

"Nice seeing you," the woman greeted her, but without much enthusiasm in her voice.

"Is something wrong?" Diane inquired, concern in her voice.

Suddenly the woman became very nervous as she twisted the straps of her small purse in her hand.

"Why do you ask?" she ventured, giving Diane a skeptical glance.

"I've noticed that you haven't seemed very happy lately. I thought that perhaps something might have happened, and I wondered if there was something I could do to help," she explained kindly, trying to ease the woman's mind.

"That's very nice of you, my dear," Sarah said, and her expression brightened. "It's just that I thought someone was following me," she went on to explain. "Probably it's only my mind playing tricks on me. You know how we old folks feel vulnerable in this city."

"Did you see anyone?"

"No, it was more of a feeling than anything else. It is pretty late, and I really shouldn't be traipsing about at this hour. It's enough to make anyone jumpy."

"I can understand that," Diane assured the woman.

"All your worrying is for nothing," Sarah told her apologetically.

"Well, you had a scare, and I'd be jumpy, too. Why don't you wait and I'll walk you to your door. I just have to say good night to someone."

"You don't have to go to any trouble on my account," the old woman insisted.

"It's no trouble. Just wait a minute . . . okay?"

"You're such a good girl," the woman said appreciatively, and smiled, looking more like her old self by the minute.

Diane smiled and hurried to Brian.

As she stepped outside, she found him leaning up against the railing of the building.

"Is she all right?" he asked.

"Just a little scared, that's all," Diane replied.

"What happened?"

"She thought someone was following her. And I told her I would walk her to her apartment."

"Good, I'll come with you," Brian announced, and straightened up.

"No, I think it's better if I go alone. You're a stranger, and I think she's still a little nervous. But, thanks."

"Are you sure?"

"I'm sure."

"Not only are you a beautiful woman, but you're also a very kind and loving one, too," he said, then kissed her.

"Thanks, I needed that."

"Thanks for tonight," he whispered, his eyes warm.

"It was all my pleasure."

"I could argue that point."

"Once a lawyer, always a lawyer," she shot back with a laugh.

"At least I'm consistent."

"I'm glad you are," she retorted, and gave him a kiss on his cheek. "Now, I'd better get back to Mrs. Dempsey."

"Sorry I took so long," Diane offered the moment she reached the woman.

"It must have been a young man," Sarah said, a twinkle in her eye.

"How'd you guess?" Diane asked, giggling, and wished that Brian were here to hear Sarah call him a young man.

"Can always tell—they put that rosy glow on a girl's face."

114

Diane smiled but could see that Sarah was still upset even though she was talking cheerfully.

The elevator doors opened and Diane guided the woman into the empty car.

Upon reaching her floor, Sarah asked, "Would you like some tea?"

Diane didn't. It was late and all she wanted to do was go home and get into bed, but she knew that Sarah, no doubt, needed company. So she responded, "That would be nice," then followed the woman into her apartment.

Sarah's home was a dimly lighted monument to the past, but Diane found it quite charming. Her living room was full of antique furniture, and some of the pieces were really unique. On one round wooden table sat a collection of pictures in old round silver frames. Obviously her family, Diane thought as she looked at the yellowed photographs of people dressed in old-fashioned clothes.

"I keep all the drapes drawn to keep out the brutal heat," Sarah explained as she scurried about, turning on some of her lamps.

"That's okay," Diane remarked, not wanting the woman to waste her electricity.

"It will only take me a few minutes to put the kettle on," she said as she scurried off to the kitchen, leaving Diane alone in the room.

Diane rested her head on the back of the sofa, and Brian came to mind. She thought about how much she had enjoyed being with him and of how he looked the moment he had told her he was falling in love with her. She couldn't remember a time when she felt happier.

Before Diane knew it, Sarah had returned, carrying a large silver tray with two white china cups and a milk pitcher and sugar bowl to match. There were also some English tea biscuits on the tray.

"I thought you might like something to eat," she explained.

Diane smiled, and even though she wasn't the least bit hungry, she politely reached out and took one of the biscuits, not wanting to disappoint the gracious woman.

Diane stayed and chatted with Sarah until she could no longer see any trace of fear on the old woman's face. When her neighbor yawned, she used the cue to excuse herself to go home.

When Diane's head finally hit the pillow, her body was tired, but her mind was wide-awake. She lay there for a while thinking that she would soon drop off, only to find it didn't happen. Finally, Diane gave up and switched on her lamp. Not knowing what else to do, she trudged toward the kitchen.

So many things had happened too quickly, and Diane didn't know what to make of it all. First, the mysterious letters and Wilding's connection with them, then Brian telling her that he was falling in love with her, and lastly, poor little Sarah being frightened out of her skin. One thing she had to admit: her life had definitely taken a drastic turn, and she didn't know if it was for the best, but she did know it wasn't boring.

She looked around the kitchen, searching for something to help her sleep. Her mother had always told her that hot milk would do the trick, so she reached inside the refrigerator and took out the milk carton. Ugh, she thought. She hated milk by itself. She only used it in her coffee, but she needed her rest and was getting desperate.

She took out a saucepan and set it on the stove. Begrudgingly, she poured the milk into the pan and frowned, not believing she was actually resorting to warm milk. She wasn't sure she would even be able to keep it down. Maybe hot chocolate would be better, she thought, then remembered that chocolate was a stimulant.

Diane had to admit that she had Brian to blame for her insomnia. She was confused. She was happy that she knew he cared about her, but she was also troubled. She even felt a little dishonest about not telling him her suspicions about Wilding. In the back of her mind, she knew she hadn't because he worked for the man, and she was afraid he could also be somehow involved. She hadn't really proved that Wilding was doing anything illegal, so she had to chalk it off to women's intuition. But the composer of the strange letters really appeared to be asking for Diane's help, and she had to believe that Wilding might have done something wrong.

Brian was Wilding's attorney, and as such, she could not confide in him. At first, she hadn't told him about the letters because she wasn't sure if they meant anything or not. But now that she really believed that Wilding might be involved in something awful, she couldn't possibly tell Brian, at least not until she had some kind of proof. Could she even trust Brian in this matter? she wondered. A shudder ran through her. That was an awful thought, but one she'd have to face. As Wilding's attorney Brian might be involved in some way. How could she love someone she didn't trust? All the unanswered questions made Diane's head spin.

She stared down at the milk in the pan.

"Yech!" she muttered. She wasn't going to deal with that and quickly poured the milk into the sink.

Instead, she turned on the television and curled up on the sofa. Sometime, somehow, Diane finally managed to fall asleep.

It wasn't until the next morning during a phone conversation with Brian, when he asked about Sarah, that it suddenly dawned on Diane that Mrs. Dempsey could be the creator of the anonymous letters. It did seem like a long shot, but it somehow fitted. The sender had to be someone from her own neighborhood who knew her, who knew where she lived and where she worked. And after seeing Mrs. Dempsey's apartment last night, even the faded stationery made sense. Diane wanted to talk to Sarah immediately. She felt she should at least follow her hunch. So when Brian told her he'd like to see her later that evening, Diane declined, telling him only that she had something to do.

Brian sounded disappointed, then told her he had to be out of town for a few days on business. So she made a date with him for early the following week. Diane was disappointed, too, but felt that in the long run maybe it was for the best. This way she had some time for herself and hopefully she would discover the meaning of the letters.

The day crept by at a snail's pace, but finally, with a sigh of relief, Diane tidied her desk and went home. She had been preoccupied the entire time with how she could broach the subject of the letters with Sarah. It wasn't every day that she accused a dear, sweet old lady of sending crank letters! She had to choose her words carefully so as not to scare or hurt the old woman by the accusation. Diane realized it was likely that her imagination was running wild again and she was wrong about Sarah sending the letters. The woman had been upset lately, and Diane wanted to make certain that she didn't add to her problems.

By the time Diane arrived home she had made up her mind to speak to Sarah and immediately went to her apartment. It wasn't like her not to call first, but she did look up her number in the phone book, only to find that it wasn't listed.

As she was about to ring Sarah's doorbell she hesitated and took a deep breath. She just hoped she wasn't making a big mistake by talking to her neighbor about the letters. But Diane's desire to know drove her on and she rang the bell.

She heard someone moving inside the apartment, and Diane assumed Sarah was home.

Finally, Sarah called out, "Who's there?"

"It's me, Diane, Mrs. Dempsey."

Diane heard the sound of a chain being removed, followed by a turn of a lock. Then the door opened and the little woman squinted as she looked up suspiciously at Diane.

"Hello," Sarah managed in a faint voice.

"I'm sorry, I hope I didn't get you at a bad time," Diane apologized, suddenly feeling that she had made a mistake, "but I wanted to talk to you."

"You do?" the woman asked, slightly uncomfortable.

Oh, no, Diane thought, here I go upsetting her again! But she knew she had come too far to turn back and couldn't just walk away from her like that.

"May I come in?" Diane asked.

"Oh, yes, of course," the woman said apologetically, and moved away from her door.

"Thank you."

"Could I get you something?" Sarah offered as soon as Diane was seated on the sofa.

"No, thank you. I don't want anything. I just wanted to talk to you."

Settling herself on an old green chair, Sarah peered at Diane.

"I don't know how to say this, but something unusual has happened to me lately."

Diane paused to get the woman's reaction. Sarah's eyes had widened.

"Now, I don't mean to upset you," she went on carefully, "but I have noticed that you've been troubled."

Diane stopped again to see if perhaps Sarah had wanted to give an explanation, but the woman offered none.

"Have any of your friends died recently?" Diane asked slowly, trying not to sound callous.

Sarah's eyes watered as though she were about to cry. Oh, no, thought Diane.

Taking a crocheted handkerchief out of her housedress, the woman stared down at it, twisting its lacy edge.

Diane felt like kicking herself. How could she have been so insensitive?

120

Slowly the old woman raised her head and looked sadly at Diane.

"I'm sorry, Sarah. Please forgive me."

"How did you know?" the old woman asked.

"Well, I don't know just how to say this," Diane started, then stopped. How could she tell her the reason she was here? The woman would think she was crazy. "I think that I've come at a bad time," Diane mumbled more to herself than Sarah.

"No, as a matter of fact, it does my heart good to see you," Sarah informed her, much to Diane's surprise.

There had been a sense of relief mixed with appreciation in the old woman's voice, which made Diane question exactly what she had meant by her words.

"I'm glad I could help," Diane said, still not understanding how she had.

"You're a nice young woman. And I didn't have anyone else to turn to," Sarah blurted out, tears threatening again.

"I don't understand," Diane admitted cautiously.

The little woman began twisting her handkerchief more rapidly.

"I had to do something. I couldn't let him get away with what he had done," the woman admitted sadly, and a tear rolled down her cheek.

Diane stared at the woman in disbelief. Did her words mean what she thought they did? Had her hunch been right on target?

"I received some letters . . ." Diane's voice trailed off. She didn't have the heart to ask the woman about them.

The old woman nodded.

Diane's eyes widened. "You know about the letters?"

The woman nodded again.

"So it *was* you," Diane said in barely a whisper.

"I knew you were bright and would figure it out," Sarah told her as a sigh of relief entered her voice. "I only hope you're not angry at me," she added nervously.

"No, of course I'm not, Sarah," Diane reassured her.

"I'm thankful for that," she said with a small smile.

"The people that were in the clippings were friends of yours—I mean, the ones from this area?"

"No, only Ruthie really was," the woman informed her as tears filled her eyes again.

"Ruth Klein?"

The old woman nodded.

"I'm sorry, Sarah," Diane said, wishing there were more that she could do.

"Thank you," she responded, bringing the handkerchief to her eyes. "It's been a great loss to me."

"I think maybe I should go," Diane said, feeling as if she were intruding upon Sarah's sorrow.

"No, please, Diane, don't go. It's good for me to get it out."

Diane waited a few moments, then she asked gently, "You didn't know the other people, is that what you said?"

"No, but I knew of them, and I knew that *that* Mr. Wilding knew them," Sarah told her, emotion filling her voice.

Mrs. Dempsey said Wilding's name with disdain,

and it didn't take much for Diane to know that Sarah didn't like the man. She had definitely made that clear.

Diane stood up and walked over to Sarah. Sitting next to the old woman, she took Sarah's small, frail hand and patted it lightly.

"I still don't understand why you wrote me those letters. I felt that you wanted me to help you, but I don't know how. You have to tell me what the problem is so I can help. Let's figure out what we can do."

Diane waited for a response, but Sarah just stared down at her lap. Diane patted her hand again.

"That's all right. I know this is difficult for you, so take your time. I'll sit and wait until you want to talk about it," Diane said kindly.

Apparently Diane's reassuring words were exactly what Sarah needed to hear, because her silence was broken as she began to talk.

"Ruthie was my best friend," she began in a shaky voice. "And I just can't get over the fact that that man was the last person to see her alive," she stated angrily.

"You mean Wilding?" Diane asked, wide-eyed.

"The very same. There was something about him that I never trusted and I told Ruthie, but she wouldn't listen. She liked him a lot, and I even think it went beyond that. I think she had a real crush on him. But she never told me that, mind you."

Diane nodded.

"Maybe it was just that he was too polished, too slick. I don't know," the old woman went on, shaking her head. "But Ruthie just adored him. He could do no wrong in her eyes. She even made him executor of her will, leaving the bulk of her money to charities to be selected by that man, of all people."

Every time Sarah had used the term *that man* it was as if she were talking about some kind of repulsive insect, Diane thought.

"I see," Diane said when Sarah paused.

"I tried to talk Ruthie out of this, but she just wouldn't pay any attention to anything I would say when it came to that Mr. Wilding. In her eyes he could do no wrong. That's when I started writing you those letters."

"I don't understand . . ."

"Well, don't you think it's strange that he knew those three women and that all of them died? Ruthie wouldn't listen to me, so I thought you could find something on that guy. That way, she would have to listen to you. She always read the obit column faithfully every day."

A tear ran down the old woman's face, and Sarah twisted her handkerchief so vigorously that Diane was afraid she'd tear it into shreds.

"Then Ruthie was gone. Went and had a heart attack, and that man was the last person to see her alive."

"She died in the morning, didn't she?" Diane asked, trying to understand how the woman knew that Wilding was the last person to see her alive.

"Yes, poor sweet, innocent thing that she was . . ." Sarah answered, her voice trailing off.

"But how did you know that Wilding was the last person to see her alive?"

"Ah," Sarah said, raising her gnarled index finger, "because I called Ruthie bright and early the morning she died to see if she wanted to do some shopping later that day. She said that she couldn't talk and was expecting a gentleman caller to have some tea with her."

"But she didn't say that the caller was Wilding, did she?"

"Didn't have to. She always referred to that man as her 'gentleman caller,' " Sarah stated with conviction as tears threatened again.

Diane sat in silence, giving Mrs. Dempsey time to control her grief. She couldn't believe what she had just heard. She had suspected Wilding of being up to something, but now Sarah was actually implicating him in her friend's death.

"Did Ruth have a history of heart problems?" she finally asked.

"She did, that's true, but I just know he had something to do with it," Sarah insisted vehemently.

Diane went over Sarah's words. She had known the woman for a while and had always found her to be a very levelheaded person. There had never been anything in her behavior that would lead Diane to believe that she was vicious or vindictive. But then again, if the woman truly believed that Wilding had been responsible for her friend's death, why hadn't she reported him to the proper authorities?

"Why didn't you go to the police with your suspicions about Wilding?" Diane asked.

"It wouldn't have made any difference. No, they'd just think I'm a crazy old woman with nothing but time on her hands and they'd laugh. That's why I knew you were the *only* one who could help me," she told her, desperation in her voice.

"Why me?"

A small smile curled up the corners of the little

woman's wrinkled mouth. "I believe in the power of the press. I've heard about Woodward and Bernstein," she announced proudly.

Sarah's words tickled Diane, making her want to laugh. But she stifled her response, not wanting to offend her. Still, she couldn't help but think how precious the dear old woman had just sounded.

"But I'm not an investigative reporter. That's what Woodward and Bernstein were. I only work on the obituary column," Diane argued.

"I know you'll do just fine. I know all about your connections," Sarah boasted, giving Diane a knowing laugh.

Diane stared in disbelief. Finally she said, "Okay." Diane knew when she was talking to a stone wall.

"Good girl, I knew I could count on you!" Sarah exclaimed, hugging herself.

"Tell me, you said Wilding had known the other people from our neighborhood who died," Diane began inquisitively.

"Yes, he did."

"I just wonder if he could have been the executor of any of the other people's wills on the list?" Diane asked, more to herself than to Sarah.

"I wouldn't put anything past him. I wouldn't put anything past that old codger," she snapped vehemently.

Diane really had to stifle her laughter this time, upon hearing Sarah's description of Wilding, especially since Mrs. Dempsey was probably quite a few years older than him.

"Well, I don't know what to do," Diane said, "but I

126

think I'll go home and do some thinking about all this."

Sarah studied Diane's face intently before she said, "Promise me you won't tell anyone about this, Diane, not even that young attorney who works for Mr. Wilding."

The little woman continued to stare at her, waiting for her answer.

Sarah was talking about Brian. Everything was getting so complicated. Diane needed to be alone to think things out.

"Okay, I won't until we have some kind of proof," Diane promised as she left the woman's apartment.

When Diane reached her door, her head was spinning. Mrs. Dempsey's news was mind-boggling! But the most important question was, Where did Brian stand in all this? Kind and loving Brian. Was it possible that she hadn't known him at all? Could the man she had grown so quickly to love, have deceived her so completely?

Now all the pieces of the puzzle were falling into place. But she wished they weren't. The reason for her strong reaction when she found out from Brian that Wilding was the executor of the dead woman's will was now painfully apparent. She must have had a premonition that whatever Wilding was up to, Brian might also be implicated.

She was glad that Brian would be out of town during the next couple of days. She needed time to sort things out. But now the possibility that the man she cared about could be involved in something as despicable as taking advantage of old, helpless people was too much for her to bear. It wasn't possible that her kind, sweet Brian could do something like that. Was it?

As the days passed, Diane contemplated discussing the latest developments in her mysterious letter case with her boss. But she finally decided to wait until she had something more concrete to go on. She had to find out if Wilding was the executor of the other people's wills. Once she had that piece of information, she would be able to decide what to do.

By the beginning of the week, she wanted to discuss her article on Wilding with John. But as it turned out, Diane didn't have any time to talk to him. She was inundated with work.

Late one afternoon, she received a call that proved to be quite disturbing. Her assistant told her that there was a woman on the line who sounded extremely upset and insisted on talking to her immediately.

The minute Diane heard the woman's voice, she knew it was Sarah.

"Diane, I'm sorry to bother you at your job, but I think he *knows!*" Sarah exclaimed in a frightened-sounding voice.

"Calm down, Sarah . . . Now, tell me, *who* knows *what?*"

"Wilding! I ran into him in the lobby this morning. I know I'm right about that man, and now he knows! He knows that I suspect him!" Sarah blurted out, clearly on the verge of hysteria.

"Don't worry, Sarah," Diane said as calmly as she could. "He probably doesn't suspect anything." Diane paused a moment, wondering what on earth she could say to the woman to calm her fears. "Listen," she finally said, "I'll come to your apartment tonight and stay with you. How would you like that?"

"You'd do that for me?" Sarah asked in a very small voice.

"Yes, of course I would," Diane answered immediately.

Her answer worked like magic. Sarah seemed quite relieved and pleased that Diane would keep her company. But the moment Diane cradled the receiver, she remembered her date with Brian.

"Oh, darn!" she muttered, wondering how she could have forgotten.

She had really looked forward to being with him and hated the idea of having to break her date. She hoped he would understand but doubted that he would.

She couldn't call Sarah back and tell her she had other plans and couldn't come. Sarah was too frightened to be left alone tonight. So, without delay, Diane dialed Brian's number to cancel their date.

The moment she heard his voice, she lost her conviction and a lump rose in her throat.

Brian immediately greeted her with, "What a pleasant surprise!"

"Did you have a good trip?"

"Yes, thanks," he said cheerfully.

"I'm sorry to be calling at the last minute like this, Brian, but I can't make it tonight," she told him quickly.

There was a long silence on the other end of the line, and Diane suspected he might be angry with her. She couldn't blame him if he was.

"You can't make it tonight?" he repeated in a monotone.

Diane knew he wanted an explanation, but she couldn't give him one. She had given Sarah her word.

"Yes, that's right. Something's come up that's really important. I hope you understand."

"What's there to understand?" he asked coolly.

She could tell by the sound of his voice that he didn't understand at all, but she thought it best not to pursue the subject. "I'm sorry," she said again.

"No sweat," he replied, not even sounding like himself.

"Could I ask you a legal question?" she asked a little timidly.

"Shoot."

"What happens if someone dies and doesn't leave a will?"

"If there are no known relatives the property will escheat to the state. Why do you ask?"

"I just wondered," she answered evasively.

"It's really foolish for a person like that not to have a will drawn up," he told her in a businesslike tone.

Sounds a lot like the line that Wilding could have used on poor Ruth, Diane thought.

"How can one find out who's the executor of a will?"

"You can look the information up in the Surrogate's Court," he replied coldly.

"Thank you," Diane said sincerely.

"Glad to be of service. The bill will be in the mail," he replied with a sarcastic edge to his voice.

Their conversation had not gone the way Diane had wanted it to, but she had to get off the phone, not wanting Brian to hear the shakiness in her voice. She didn't want him to know that she suspected him of being involved with Wilding. Brian had, after all, drawn up Ruth's will.

Diane's heart sank. She felt worse than she could ever have imagined. She knew she had hurt Brian by not offering him a real explanation for canceling their date. But under the circumstances, she didn't know what else to do. If she had told him she had to see someone about an important matter, he might not have believed her.

Well, what was done was done, she mused, and began to make a list of what she had to do before spending the night with Sarah.

CHAPTER SEVEN

The instant Brian set the receiver on its hook, the full extent of his anger hit him. Talk about a woman getting under his skin! She had gotten all the way to his arteries this time, and his blood was boiling.

It was the second time in a row she'd shot him down. Was she playing hard to get, or what? She hadn't even offered any kind of explanation for breaking the date. And he had gotten too angry to ask her for one. Diane's insensitive treatment of him was just too much for his ego to bear.

During the time he had been away from her, he had missed her terribly. He had really looked forward to seeing her again. She didn't even know that he had planned a special evening for her, just to show her how much he cared. He had bought tickets for a Broadway show and made dinner reservations at her favorite restaurant. Now, everything was kaput, thanks to Diane's last-minute cancellation.

Something was terribly wrong here, he thought, placing his elbow on his desk and resting his chin on his hand. The last time they were together they had a wonderful time. At least, *he* had a wonderful time. But then, for no apparent reason, she had insisted on going home, instead of staying the night with him. Afterward, she had seen an old woman, then they had parted. From that point on, she had been unavailable and hadn't shown one ounce of concern for his feelings.

Maybe he had been too soft on her. Maybe he had let her know too soon how much he cared for her. He had never been so honest and giving in his life, and it hadn't gotten him anywhere. Perhaps now he was getting his payback for previous relationships that he had not worked at very hard, he thought. At least he had always been right up front about his intentions, unlike Diane. He still couldn't understand her actions.

Well, sitting here and brooding was definitely not going to make him feel any better, Brian reasoned. He had to plan his next move. And the big question was, What was he going to do tonight? He opened his desk drawer and took out a small white envelope that contained theater tickets to a Broadway hit. He had wanted to see the play, and it annoyed him tremendously to think the tickets might go to waste.

He tapped the envelope absentmindedly against the edge of his mahogany desk as he tried to figure out what he wanted to do. It irritated the hell out of him to have to give the seats away. No, he wouldn't do that, he suddenly decided as his anger surged again. He wouldn't give her the satisfaction of sitting at home alone while she was out—God knows where and with God knows who. He could always go through his address book and make a few calls to see who was available. That way, the next time he talked to her, he would be able to mention what she had missed.

He stuck the tickets into his jacket pocket and glanced at his watch. It was still early enough in the afternoon so that he just might get lucky and find someone available. He took his address book out of his drawer and flipped through the pages.

Later that evening, Brian sat alone in his apartment. The evening, from start to finish, had been a disaster. He didn't pay attention to any of the play, he couldn't remember what the food had tasted like, and he had a hard time carrying on any kind of sensible conversation. All he could think about was Diane, and what she was doing. He had dropped his date off early and had come straight home. He fixed himself an extradry martini and decided to put Diane out of his mind, once and for all. She had trampled on his feelings and ruined his night. It was time to end their relationship.

But as the night wore on and he had one drink too many, he decided he had let her get away with much too much. He sat down on the couch, glanced over at the phone, and took a swig of his drink. He removed his shoe and tossed it across the room. As he struggled with the other shoe, his anger took hold, and he decided he had to call her one last time to tell her off.

Brian took a large gulp of his martini to steady his rage. He wanted to make certain that he got it all out, that he let her know what she had done to him. That's the least he could do for the rest of the boys who might be taken in by her alluring eyes and perfect legs. That way, the next time she had some poor, unsuspecting guy in her vise, maybe she might think twice before squeezing her next victim.

With great difficulty, Brian crawled over to the phone and grabbed the receiver. It took a few minutes for his eyes to focus, then he dialed her number, punching the buttons with unnecessary force.

The phone rang several times. What if she weren't home? To be robbed of his revenge would surely do him in. But just as he was about to hang up, someone picked up the phone.

Brian barely heard the word "Hello" as he nearly shouted, "You're not going to get away with this!"

"What!" came a startled voice.

"Don't play dumb—you know what you've done!" he charged.

"Who's this?"

Suddenly it registered through his stupor that the voice on the other end sounded strange.

"Diane?" he asked meekly, hoping he hadn't made a mistake.

"You've got the wrong number!" came an angry voice, and the receiver was slammed down in his ear.

Brian stared at the phone. He felt like an idiot. But he wasn't about to be put off; he was more determined than ever to reach her.

He looked at the phone and very carefully and very slowly punched in each number. He let the phone ring a dozen times before he got it into his thick head that she wasn't home. He slammed the receiver down. How could she do this to him? He thought for a few minutes and then decided that he would continue to call until he got her.

He switched on the television and turned to *The Tonight Show.* He needed a little comic relief. He slowly sipped his drink and stared blankly at the screen in between calls to Diane.

Sometime after one, he fell asleep. He abruptly awoke with a humming in his ears and the sound of the television blaring. It took him a few seconds to

135

realize that the humming sound was the dial tone. He had the receiver to his ear and had fallen asleep still trying to reach Diane. It was the middle of the night and she still hadn't come home!

Brian raised himself up slowly but only managed to get to a sitting position. His body ached from being cramped into the small confines of his couch, and even though he had put the receiver down, his head felt like the humming would never stop.

He moaned. Nothing had worked out the way he had planned and he was miserable. He looked at his watch. It was three in the morning. Just for good measure, he dialed her number. There was still no answer, and Brian gripped the receiver tightly. She *had* to be with a guy, and she had told him she wasn't involved with anyone. But then again, for Diane sleeping around might not have anything to do with being involved. He just might have been one of many conquests for her. The guy she was with tonight must be someone special, he told himself, because she *was* spending the night with him.

Brian knew he was jealous, but the rage he had thought he would feel wasn't there. Instead, he felt sad and lonely and—hurt. He would have easily preferred to be angry.

He rose slowly and walked over to the picture window. He glanced out at the Queensborough Bridge. Brian thought about the night he had brought Diane here and how he had made love to her. She had the most incredibly soft skin, and the way she had responded to his touch had driven him wild. She was the most sensuous woman he had ever known.

He had told her he loved her and then she had disappeared from his life. Perhaps his admission had frightened her. But worse yet, maybe she hadn't had the heart to tell him she didn't share his feelings and would never be able to return his love.

Knowing that the deck was stacked against him, he decided he should admit defeat and walk away. But one thing he did know: first he had to confront Diane and find out why she had treated him so unkindly. Then he could walk away. His pride wouldn't allow him to do otherwise.

When Brian dragged himself into the bathroom the following morning and saw his haggard appearance in the mirror, his anger once again surfaced. He couldn't believe that he'd allowed a woman to do this to him. He turned swiftly and headed for the phone. He dialed her number. But to his chagrin, there was still no answer. His anger consumed him, and he knew he had to see her—he had to get everything off his chest. Never had he been treated so unjustly, and his rage was turning him into a person he hardly knew.

He would never have believed that he was stooping to what he was about to do, but he couldn't help himself. He had to see her, and the only way he could was to hope to catch her at her apartment before she went to work. She had to change clothes and get ready for the office, didn't she? he reasoned. He would stand outside her building and wait for her!

The instant Diane awoke, everything was clear. She had to talk to Brian. She had to tell him why she had broken two dates with him without giving him any explanation. She had to find out once and for all whether he was involved with helping Wilding take advantage of helpless, defenseless widows. This not knowing was killing her. She had to confront him and find out if Brian really was the man she hoped he was. When she told him about her suspicions, she would watch him very carefully. All it would take was one nervous twitch along his jaw, eyes that couldn't look directly into hers, or a twist to his sensuous mouth— and then she would know. With her decision made, she felt like a great weight had been lifted from her shoulders.

She had spent a pleasant evening with Mrs. Dempsey and calmed the old woman's fears. Diane had told her that she could check the records to find out if Wilding had been the executor of any of the other deceased's wills. Sarah had seemed pleased with this information, and they had had a wonderful dinner. They both had appointments the next day and had gone to bed early.

But Diane had a hard time sleeping. She had missed Brian, and felt terrible about the way she had treated him. She should have given him a reason for her change of plans. He had been angry. She hadn't been able to overlook the sarcasm in his voice, and she wondered how to approach him now. He might after all, not even want to talk to her. But by the time she fell asleep she was determined to find a way to make him understand.

Now as she rushed to her apartment to change for work Diane felt relieved. She knew she could not go on with this charade any longer. She would tell him everything, even about Wilding and her fears that Brian, himself, could be somehow involved. She had to find out once and for all that he wouldn't do anything underhanded. She could no longer live, not knowing. She had to find out—one way or another. She loved the man, and to think he could be up to something shady was tearing her apart. She would talk to Sarah first and explain her situation. She would help the woman understand why she had to tell Brian about their suspicions of Wilding.

With her decision made, she quickly changed into fresh clothes, reapplied her makeup, and then dashed out the door to the elevators.

Once downstairs, she strode across the lobby and through the large glass doors. Finally her feet hit the sidewalk. It was getting late, and she'd better hurry.

As she rushed along she thought she recognized a figure standing at the corner. She did a double take. It was Brian! Her body automatically tensed, but her step didn't falter as she continued to walk toward him. She knew he might be angry with her, but perhaps this chance meeting might break the ice.

"Fancy meeting you," he quipped before she had a chance to say a word.

She was instantly taken aback by the coldness in his voice and the somber look in his eyes, but she tried to act very nonchalantly. "We have to stop meeting like this and go out to dinner."

"That way, you'd get another chance to cancel at the last minute," he replied, his voice full of sarcasm.

Diane stared at him. It obviously wasn't going to be easy for her to make things right with him. She could see that. "I guess I deserve that."

"You're damn right, you do," he shot back.

"Look, I'm sorry, Brian. I know how things must seem to you, but I really do care a lot about you. It's

139

just that I have something to work out. And once I do, I'll explain everything to you." Diane suddenly felt uneasy about questioning Brian about Wilding. She didn't want to make him even angrier than he was.

"I thought you said you weren't involved with anyone," he accused abruptly, as if he hadn't heard a word she'd said.

"I *just* apologized," she said, not liking the way he had just dismissed her words.

"Well, *are* you?" he pressed, peering down at her.

"Am I what?" she asked, now getting annoyed herself.

"Are you involved with anyone? I mean, do you have something serious going with anyone else?"

"No. I told you, there's no one else in my life."

"Where were you last night?"

"That's none of your business," she snapped angrily, wondering why she hadn't seen this nasty side of him before.

"That's where you're wrong!" he almost shouted.

"This is silly," she said, shaking her head, then laughing. "I have to get to work."

Diane started to move, but Brian blocked her way.

"I know you didn't come home last night."

Diane stared at him in disbelief. "What did you say?"

"You heard me. I know you were with someone!" he exclaimed, raising his voice.

"So, you were snooping on me again!"

"I thought all I had to do was ask and you'd give me the answers. You seem to change your rules to fit your needs. Where were you?" he demanded.

"I don't like to be interrogated!" she yelled.

140

"And I don't like to be lied to!"

Diane glared at him and retorted, "I don't know what you're talking about."

"I bet you don't."

"I didn't lie to you."

"That's a matter of opinion."

"You can think what you like, but I didn't lie to you," she said.

"You're not going to tell me where you were, huh?" he asked, as if he were giving her some kind of last chance.

"I don't owe you any explanation," she returned stubbornly.

"Oh, no, you don't? We had a date. I made special plans and you canceled without any explanation. I think you owe me something."

"What are you talking about?"

"I had tickets to a play. I wanted to surprise you."

"Oh, Brian, I'm sorry," she said as a pained expression crossed her face.

"Don't worry. The other woman enjoyed it immensely," he told her cruelly.

Diane stared at him, too hurt for words.

"You owe me an explanation," he repeated.

Quietly Diane said, "I can't tell you right now."

"So that's the way it is. Fine!" Brian exclaimed, and without a further word, left in a huff.

Diane just stood there on the sidewalk, watching his tall frame disappear down the street. She could hardly believe what had happened.

How could things have gotten so badly messed up? she wondered in dismay. Why did he have to throw another woman in her face! And how did he know she hadn't come home last night? He must have called, she reasoned.

So he really had been checking up on her and he obviously had been lying in wait for her this morning. He couldn't have been there to see Wilding; it was much too early for that. She didn't like the idea of his standing on street corners waiting for her, but at the same time, she couldn't totally blame him. She hadn't been open with him and he had sensed that. She should have tried to give him some kind of explanation for not seeing him, but he had been so belligerent that she had simply fought back. Diane had never seen this side of Brian before, and she began to wonder if this might be a regular routine with him. Maybe his lurking around and his seedy behavior was a tip-off to the inner workings of a criminal mind. Her worst fears could be confirmed. Perhaps he wasn't what he appeared to be at all.

Diane's feet automatically started moving, but her mind stayed stuck in one spot. She didn't know what to believe. Who was he? This man who had so successfully climbed over her walls and stolen her heart. Saint or sinner? She had to know. She really loved him, but there were so many things clouding the issue.

As she walked toward work Diane tossed her problem around in her head. She had to do something, and the only way to work things out with Brian was to find out once and for all if there were any truth in her and Sarah's suspicions concerning Wilding. She knew she could no longer confront Brian about the problem. The first thing she had to do was talk to Sarah about Brian and then maybe see if she could persuade her to stay with friends out of town. That way, Diane wouldn't have to worry about her being upset by Wilding again.

On Friday, Diane was finally able to take time off from work. She rode the subway train all the way to lower Manhattan to city hall and the Surrogate's Court. Inside the Record Room, she looked up each of the deceased's names in the index file. Once she had obtained their file numbers, she had to fill out a requisition form for each file number. After she did this, she waited as the clerk behind the desk brought out the entire file on the person named on the form. She had to review each file separately.

Ruth Klein's name was not listed in the file. She asked the clerk about this. She was told that because the death was recent, she had to go to the Probate Department. Records were filed there first before they came down to the Record Room. She was also informed that the will might not be probated yet; it was also possible that the executor may not have initiated a probate proceeding yet. In that case, the will wouldn't be there for her to see.

When Diane received the first file, she couldn't believe the amount of information that was made available to her. Included in the folder were the Petition for Probate, the Last Will and Testament, and miscellaneous documents. Her heart began to pound when she discovered that Wilding had been named executor of each will. She shouldn't have been surprised, but she was. Diane was even more surprised to discover that in each will the very same charities had been named. She thought this odd but didn't know exactly what it meant.

Diane went over the third will carefully to see if she

143

could discover anything else. Suddenly she realized that another law firm, other than Brian's, had been listed on the back cover attached to the will. Then it dawned on her: Dwyer, Lytle and Maxwell had only just recently started handling Wilding's affairs. So Brian most likely was not involved! She felt elated!

She quickly looked over the other legal documents that had been filed in the Surrogate's Court to see what law firm had handled these for Wilding. But to her surprise, no attorney's legal backs were attached to the papers, only a plain blue back with Wilding's name showing he had appeared *pro se*. Strange, she thought. She didn't know exactly what that meant, but at least Brian's name wasn't on any of the legal papers. She assumed that was a good sign.

Diane decided that she would like to be able to go over the wills at her leisure. She approached the clerk and asked, "How could I get a copy of these?"

"Do you want them certified?"

"Why would I want that?" she inquired, not understanding his question.

"People normally do that so there won't be any question about the validity of the document," the tall man explained.

Couldn't hurt, she thought, and replied, "Yes, that's what I want."

"Okay, I'll have the certified copies ordered for you."

After she finished getting all the information she needed, she went to the Record Room to check on Ruth Klein's will, only to find it hadn't been recorded yet. Then she spent the rest of the afternoon at the library, going through back issues of papers, looking for some information on Wilding. There were some articles on his late wife, Debra Jennings, and her work with numerous charitable organizations, but not too much on Wilding himself.

Finally, when she'd almost given up and her neck and her eyes were killing her, Diane found a small article about how Wilding had been let go from a very prestigious brokerage firm some years ago. The article had been placed in the back of the paper so as not to draw much attention to it. No reason for his dismissal had been given. It was simply written that Wilding had been replaced as financial adviser by another man. Finding this article gave Diane the idea that perhaps Wilding had been fired for doing something underhanded. She wondered if he could have somehow embezzled monies from the company and if he were now in financial straits. It seemed unlikely because his late wife had apparently inherited a fortune. By the time Diane left the library she was more baffled than ever.

She had had the nagging feeling all day that she was forgetting something, but it wasn't until her feet hit the concrete that she realized what it was. Today was the day for her haircut! She glanced at her watch. If she hurried, she could still make her appointment.

Luckily the salon was not too far from the library, and Diane had only a few blocks to walk. The extremely modern Trump Tower was crowded as Diane made her way to the elevators. When she reached Christian's, the stylist looked at his watch and glared at her. She smiled apologetically as she quickly slipped into a smock.

As she watched her shorn locks fall to the floor, a brilliant idea popped into her head. Why not introduce herself to Wilding and tell him that she wanted to do an article on him? Then she'd be able to pump him for information. She had already talked to her boss about the possibility of her writing the story on Wilding, so she wouldn't be lying. She could offer to do the article on a "spec" basis. That way, she wouldn't necessarily be deceiving Wilding if it weren't printed. She was about to be given a great opportunity to further her career, and she would take full advantage of it.

"Well, what do you think?" the hairstylist asked, breaking into her thoughts.

Diane gazed at her reflection in the mirror. Her auburn hair was cut shoulder length, giving her a more youthful, trendy look. She shook her head and noted how bouncy and shiny her hair was. Funny, she looked younger, but since she had had that fight with Brian, she felt ancient. In the few days since their stormy sidewalk argument, she had lost her enthusiasm for most things. The only thing that had kept her going was her desire to find out about Wilding.

The stylist handed her a mirror, and she turned in her chair so she could see the back of the haircut. She smiled. "It's perfect. Thank you," she murmured.

"That other hairdo simply didn't do you justice," he said, proudly touching the ends of his masterpiece.

"I have to agree," she replied pleasantly, and then wondered if Brian would like her new hairdo.

He had not called, nor did she think that he would. She had actually spent only a short time with him, but he had filled a void in her life. She hadn't realized this earlier, but it was now painfully apparent: she missed him. But the worst part of it all was late at night when she was in her bed alone, thinking that she'd never

146

know his touch again. The only thing she could hope for was to get the evidence she needed to prove that Wilding was somehow swindling these old women out of their money and show it to Brian. Then, just maybe, he would be able to understand her actions.

When Diane arrived home, she decided she'd have to find a way to "accidentally on purpose" run into Wilding. She smiled, realizing she was doing exactly what she had accused Brian of doing—hanging out in hallways. Well, it had to be done, she decided.

The instant she entered the lobby, she headed for her mailbox and suddenly remembered that that was where everything started, where she met Brian and discovered the mysterious letters.

She opened the box and started flipping through her junk mail and bills. Every so often, she looked anxiously around, hoping to catch a glimpse of Wilding. As she waited she wondered how such a nice-looking and polite older man like him could do anything dishonest. Doubts flooded her mind. Maybe she had been wrong about him all along. Just because he was an executor of a will or two didn't make him a villain. And Sarah's grief over the loss of her friend could certainly have colored her opinion of the man.

Diane suddenly felt very silly standing there pretending to be going through her mail and glancing over her shoulder every other second. She didn't know what caused her sudden rush of doubts, but rather than stand there and feel more and more uncomfortable, Diane immediately fled to the security of her apartment.

But later Diane had to admit that her last-minute jitters had to do more with her inability to accept the worst about Brian than with any doubts she might have about her feelings for Wilding. Her fears really made her face the reality of having to forget Brian, of losing him. Once Diane knew what the problem was, she felt a lot better. At least she wasn't dealing with any ghosts. She felt a lot better on one level, but on another, she was also more acutely aware of what the consequences could be if she continued to pursue the truth. The truth could separate her from Brian forever. But she had come this far and had given her word to her friend. No, she wouldn't turn back now.

Diane spent the next few days working, her early evenings hoping to run into Wilding, and her nights missing Brian. Finally, late one afternoon, she couldn't take the waiting any longer and decided to pay Mr. Wilding a visit at his home. She had hoped to make their meeting seem very casual, but since she had discovered the same charities in all the wills, she couldn't put off talking to him. She didn't like the idea of just barging in on him, but she didn't know what else to do. He wasn't listed in the phone book, and he didn't have an office—he worked out of his home. Brian was the only person she knew who could introduce her to him, and she certainly wasn't going to call him.

With an air of purpose, Diane rushed toward the elevators. It was do or die with her now. The doors opened and Diane hurried toward them without really looking where she was going. She caught herself just as she almost bumped into a man walking out.

"Oh, I'm sorry," she apologized, then realized the man was Wilding.

"Quite all right. No harm done," he politely assured her.

"Mr. Wilding, you're just the person I wanted to see!" she exclaimed, unable to contain her delight.

"I am?" he asked, raising his brows in a puzzled expression.

"Yes, you are. I guess I should explain myself."

"Please do," he urged as they moved away from the elevator.

"First of all, I'd like to introduce myself. I'm Diane Morrison and a neighbor of yours," she announced, offering him her hand.

He took her hand and shook it with surprising gentleness. "And I'm very happy to meet you at last. We've been bumping into each other. At least now, I'll know your name. But you look different. What is it?" he asked as he studied her face. "Your hair?"

"Yes, I just got it cut," Diane told him, surprised that he had remembered her after all.

"Quite stunning," Wilding said appreciatively.

"Thank you," she replied, feeling slightly uneasy.

"A beautiful woman should always be complimented," he went on in a charming way.

A smile automatically crossed Diane's face as she thought what a smooth talker this man was. She could readily see the appeal he would have for any woman. But she was on her guard, and it would take a lot more than a few pretty words to pull the wool over her eyes.

"The reason I wanted to see you," she quickly went on, "is that I work for the *New York Press,* and I would like to do a feature on you."

"On me?" the man asked, truly surprised but obviously flattered.

"Yes, on you," she repeated, watching the man's ego take over. The trap had been baited. Would the rat like a little cheese?

"I don't understand," he said.

"You're a very important man in the community, and I think many people would like to know more about you. Are you interested?" she asked, coming right to the point.

"I'm very flattered, thank you."

I bet you are, she thought.

"I think we should get together and discuss the possibility," he said. "How would you like to come to a little party I'm throwing at my apartment tomorrow night?"

"Tomorrow night?" she repeated, shocked that it had been so easy.

"Too short a notice?" he asked, a little disappointed.

"No, not at all . . . Yes, I'd love to come, thank you."

"I'm delighted," he replied and smiled.

"What shall I wear? Is it casual or formal?"

"Wear what you like. Some of the women will be wearing cocktail dresses."

Diane nodded. "All right, I'll keep that in mind."

"We could discuss what type of article you intend to write, and we'll get to know each other a little better. The party starts at eight. I look forward to seeing you."

"I look forward to it, too," she agreed.

"And I'm looking forward to getting to know you better," he said. Then he took her hand and kissed it.

Diane smiled awkwardly. Wilding was really being very nice, and here she was, setting him up to get the goods on him. She didn't feel very good about that and withdrew her hand as quickly as she could without seeming impolite.

"Good-bye," she said, and moved toward the elevators.

"See you later," he called after her, and turned to leave the building.

After he left, Diane felt elated. Things couldn't have worked better. He had actually invited her into his home. She was surprised at how easy he was to talk to and felt a little guilty about what she was up to. But then Sarah and Brian came to mind, and she knew that she had to go to Wilding's penthouse tomorrow night to find out anything she could about him and those charities that had been listed in the wills.

The trap had been set! The article appealed to Wilding's ego. Perhaps he didn't have anything to hide. Or maybe he was just too confident. Whatever the reason, everything had worked flawlessly.

As she neared her floor a disturbing thought suddenly gnawed at her. All this time she thought she'd been the clever one . . . Would she be stepping into the spider's web like an unsuspecting fly?

CHAPTER EIGHT

It was time for Wilding's party before Diane knew it. She had gone to a local boutique to buy something special for the occasion. She had decided on a blue silk dress with a modern design and a jacket to match. As she walked down the hallway toward Wilding's penthouse she had to admit her very jazzy dress and new haircut did wonders for her appearance.

She reached his door, took a deep breath, and rang the buzzer. She could hear soft music and the murmur of voices as she waited. Suddenly the door opened and a very dignified looking white-haired butler peered out at her.

"Hello. I'm Diane Morrison," she said quickly.

"Right this way, miss," the man replied in a formal tone.

Diane followed the slightly stoop-shouldered man through a long corridor into a large room filled with guests. The men were all dressed in dark well-tailored suits, and the women wore beautiful dresses and sparkling jewelry.

His task done, the butler left her side, and Diane was alone. She felt a little self-conscious, wishing that she knew someone, as her eyes searched the room for the host. A waiter approached her with a large silver tray containing glasses filled with champagne. He offered her a glass and she took one.

Diane sipped her champagne as she continued to look over the crowd. She would have given anything to be in her own apartment, watching television or reading a good book. She had to force herself to remember why she was there.

Suddenly her gaze fell upon the back of a head that looked a lot like Brian's. It couldn't be! she thought. She had never imagined that he could be there. But why hadn't she? He was, after all, Wilding's attorney. Her heart raced and her hand felt clammy against the cool glass. Could two people possibly have exactly the same shade of blond hair? She started to turn, but it was too late. Unfortunately the head had swung around and *he* was facing her. His dark eyes impaled her.

Diane froze. She went through a whole gamut of emotions, from happiness to vulnerability to fear—and then finally, to sadness. There was no warmth in his eyes, no sign that he cared, nothing that reminded her of what they had shared together. She wanted to flee. She could no longer endure the pain—the pain of seeing a look of contempt on his handsome face.

Diane broke away from his glare. She stood motionless, not knowing what to do. Luckily she saw Wilding walking toward her.

Taking her hand the minute he reached her, he exclaimed, "I'm glad you could make it! You look very lovely, Diane."

"Thank you. Your party is very festive," she replied, not knowing what else to say, still feeling shaken by seeing Brian.

"Come, let me introduce you around," Wilding suggested.

"Okay," she responded, taking a quick glance back to see if Brian was still watching her.

He wasn't. He had moved and she didn't know where he was.

Diane followed Wilding around, and he introduced her to some very nice people. She couldn't help but wonder if any of the older women here were widows and would be his next victims.

Just when she felt she was in the clear and started to relax, Brian suddenly popped up alongside them.

"Oh, Brian, I'd like you to meet one of my dear neighbors," Wilding began the minute he noticed Brian.

Brian's lips twisted into a cynical smile. Diane tensed, not knowing what he was up to.

"I've already met Ms. Morrison," Brian said.

"You have?" Wilding asked, surprised.

Diane glared at Brian. She hadn't cared for the sarcastic edge to his voice.

"Yes, we know each other," Diane quickly interjected before Brian had a chance to answer.

Wilding smiled at Brian. "Then perhaps you know that she might do an article on me," the older man announced rather proudly.

A disbelieving look came into Brian's eyes, and Diane felt as if her heart had almost stopped beating. Would Brian tell Wilding the truth about her?

"No, she didn't mention that," he returned flatly.

"I'm very flattered that such a beautiful woman would find me that interesting," Wilding went on, seeming not to notice Brian's cool manner.

154

"She's full of surprises," Brian remarked offhandedly.

Wilding eyed him closely.

"She certainly surprised me, if that's what you mean," the elder man declared.

"Yes, of course," Brian added more civilly.

Someone suddenly caught Wilding's eye and he excused himself and turned quickly, leaving Diane alone to face Brian.

The minute the older man was out of earshot, Brian exclaimed, "Alone at last!"

Diane ignored him.

"I see you made some changes," he went on.

Diane looked at him. She couldn't miss his derogatory intent. Not wanted to start a scene, she remained silent.

"Now everything makes sense, all your questions about Wilding," he said accusingly.

"I don't know what you're insinuating," she came back, wanting to pin him to the wall.

"You don't have to pull your sweet, little innocent routine with me. I fell for it once, but I can assure you that I never make the same mistake twice."

"Are you finished?" she asked, trying to control her temper.

"You must be kidding. I've only just begun."

"Well, I don't have to stand here and take this from you!"

"So, you were only using me so you could get an article on Wilding! You must have been disappointed when I didn't introduce you to him. But I see that you've managed by yourself, very well. But then, sneaky operators always do well!"

155

"What!"

"You heard me! Save your acting ability for Wilding, your next fall guy!"

"What's that supposed to mean?" she demanded, not believing Brian's audacity.

"Oh, I suppose you don't have the foggiest idea," he said in a condescending tone.

"No, I don't."

"I told you I loved you, and you dropped me like a hot potato," he spat out.

"That's not so!"

"Then why don't you tell me what *is so,*" Brian demanded.

Tears welled up in her eyes, and she knew she had to leave. This wasn't the time or the place to pour her heart out to him. Nor did she want to, not the way he was treating her.

"I don't want to talk to you when you're acting this way," she stated firmly.

"Oh, I see. You want me to treat you with kid gloves," he said, raising his voice.

"Lower your voice," she ordered, and looked nervously around to see if anyone had overheard them.

"What's the matter? The truth getting to you?"

"Look, I don't have to stand here and be insulted. Now, if you'll excuse me, I'd like to go and talk to civilized people." She started to walk away.

"When things get tough, you just split," he accused, and his words halted her exit.

With as much dignity and self-control as she could muster, she said, "Well, I'm not going to stand here and listen to you make a fool of yourself."

Before he could say a word, she had turned on her

heel and left, but not before she caught the look of pain in his dark eyes.

Brian's presence at the party had ruined everything for Diane. Try as she may, she couldn't get his nastiness and haunting look out of her mind. And every time she tried to approach Wilding, Brian always managed to be somewhere very close, making it very difficult for her to talk to him.

Finally she decided it would be best if she left. She couldn't accomplish her goal, and she couldn't bear to stand around and watch Brian flirt with all the attractive women. She approached Wilding, thanked him for inviting her, and very quietly left.

Once she closed her apartment door, the tears she'd been fighting to hold back flooded down her cheeks. It was over between her and Brian, and she felt terrible.

Suddenly there was a loud banging on her door. Before she had a chance to wonder who it was, she heard Brian's voice.

"Open up! I know you're in there!" he yelled, and banged some more.

The last thing on earth she wanted to do was let him in, but neither did she want her neighbors to call the police.

"Keep your pants on!" she yelled back, and wiped away her tears before rushing to the door and opening it.

"What the hell do you think you're doing, coming banging on my door like that!" she snapped at him.

Her vehemence momentarily threw him off the track, and he stared at her, his mouth wide open.

"Well, what do you want?" she demanded angrily.

"I want to know what's with you."

"Come in. I don't want you to wake the neighbors. Some people do sleep at this hour, you know," she said as she backed away from the door.

"Okay, but I want you to know I'm not letting you off so lightly this time!"

"What does that mean? Do you think you scare me?"

"No, I don't think anything would scare you. You're hard as nails!"

"Get to why you're here!" she ordered, trying her best to hold herself together but feeling as if she could fall apart at any moment.

"You used me! You are the most secretive person I've ever met. All the time I thought you cared for me you were just hoping to meet Wilding. If that's what you wanted, why didn't you just tell me? At least, I should have been warned that you liked the grandfatherly type."

"Wilding is very charming and dignified and could run circles around you any day," she retorted, wanting to hurt him in some way.

"And what am I—chopped liver?" he shot back.

"*You* said it. I didn't."

Silence fell over them, and Diane had a moment to think about what she had just said to him. She looked at him and could see the vulnerability in his eyes, and she suddenly wondered why they were doing this to each other. He must have cared, or he wouldn't have been so hurt.

Almost in a whisper, Diane said, "Brian, I didn't mean that, but I just got so mad."

"Diane, what has happened to us? I loved you."

Diane's heart stopped. He had said he loved her. He'd used the past tense.

"Diane, would you please tell me what happened?" he pleaded.

She knew she still loved him, and there was no longer any reason to hold back the truth.

Diane sighed wearily. It wasn't going to be easy, but it had to be done. "I think you'd better sit down. I have something to tell you," she said in a very tired voice.

Without saying a word, Brian did exactly as he was told. Once seated on the sofa, he looked up at her questioningly. "Well?"

"This isn't easy," she began.

"I don't know what could be worse than what I've already been through," he stated simply.

She stared at him. It was true—his handsome face did seem tired and worn.

"Okay, I don't know how you're going to take this, but I'm going to tell you everything."

"It's about time."

"Look, I don't need any of that," she warned.

"I'm sorry. Please go ahead."

"The day I met you, I received an anonymous letter."

"You did?" he asked in a surprised voice.

"Yes, I did. The letter said that I didn't know what was happening in my neighborhood and that I should help innocent victims from being preyed upon."

"I don't understand what this has to do with us," he interrupted.

"You will. But please don't interrupt me. You

159

wanted to hear my story, and if you keep interrupting me, I may not have the courage to finish it."

"All right, I won't interrupt again."

"For a lawyer, that's a little hard to do, isn't it?" she asked with a small smile.

Brian smiled in return.

"I guess you've got my number," he declared. And Diane thought she heard a note of affection in his voice.

"Anyway, that's another reason why I was so preoccupied the day we went for breakfast," Diane explained. "The second time I received an anonymous letter was when we passed through my lobby and I stopped and got my mail. Do you remember when the clippings fell to the floor and you helped me pick them up?"

"Yes."

"Well, one of those clippings was an article about your company and Wilding. The others were copies of my obituary column."

She paused, knowing she was reaching the hard part. Brian was staring at her intently.

"To make a long story short, I discovered that it was Sarah Dempsey who had sent me the anonymous letters, and that she thought Stephen Wilding had something to do with the death of her friend Ruth Klein," she said quickly, then took a deep sigh of relief.

"That's the woman who died recently. The one whose will I delivered to Wilding?" he asked.

"Yes."

"Your friend Sarah thought Wilding had something to do with her death?" he inquired skeptically.

"Yes, she did."

The sudden look upon Brian's face was not what she had expected, nor what she had wanted to see. A warning cloud had settled upon his features.

"What the hell are you saying?" he demanded as his mouth took on an unpleasant twist.

"I suppose I didn't explain it very well," she answered nervously.

"No, you didn't."

"Well, the clippings of my obituary column were of three women from this area, not including Ruth Klein. I went to the Surrogate's Court, and I looked up their wills and found out that Wilding was the executor for all of them."

"Now everything makes sense," he declared cynically.

"I knew you wouldn't understand."

"You haven't told me anything. I don't understand what any of this has to do with us. And if you're insinuating that Wilding has done something illegal, that's the most preposterous thing I've ever heard. You've got nothing on him except that he was the executor of a few women's wills."

"It's just not that, Brian. The charities listed in all the wills are the same."

"What *are* you saying?"

"Maybe he somehow got their money that was supposed to go to the charities," she answered, not really knowing if that was probable or not."

"That's crazy. Besides, what motive would he have?"

"Maybe he was broke," she offered lamely.

"Diane, you're just grasping at straws. And now you want to do an article on him. I suppose you're planning to expose him as a con man. You'd do anything to further your career, wouldn't you? Even if it meant discrediting a kind old man who has done nothing but help other people," he stated with disgust.

"Oh, great! Before he was the grandfather type, and now he's your buddy!"

"And you're just out for a story!"

"And who the hell are you to judge me?" she asked through clenched teeth.

"The guy who works with Wilding!"

"You're too emotionally involved. Look at the evidence!" she shouted.

"What evidence?" he shouted louder.

"Well, what about his charities—are they legitimate?" she asked, doing her best to maintain control.

Brian's eyes narrowed as he glared at her, but he didn't say anything.

"Or are you afraid I might be right, and you'd lose a little business?" Diane demanded triumphantly.

"So, now we're finally getting around to what this is all about! You think I'm involved with something seedy, don't you?"

The intense gaze to his eyes pierced through to her very soul.

"Is *that* why you dumped me?" he asked in a low, frighteningly calm voice.

"It's the reason I couldn't tell you what was going on. I wanted to tell you, but I was afraid you wouldn't understand—and I was right: you don't. I also promised Sarah I wouldn't tell anyone until we had some kind of proof."

"Just what kind of proof do you have?" he demanded.

"That's just the problem—I don't. It's more of a gut feeling."

"Why are you telling me now?"

"Because I don't think you're involved."

"So, at one point you *did* think I was involved?"

"Yes, it crossed my mind that you could somehow have been implicated if Wilding had found a way to con the women out of their money. You were, after all, the one who drew up Ruth Klein's will."

"Well, little lady, I'm going to get your facts straight for you and prove you wrong," he declared, and quickly stood up.

"I don't believe you're involved, Brian. That's why I told you," she explained in a low voice.

"It's a shame you couldn't have trusted me a little in the beginning. I think it's too late now, wouldn't you say?"

"No, I wouldn't," she said stubbornly.

"Truth and honesty are very important ingredients in a relationship. And when you don't have either one, you don't have anything."

"Are you saying it's over between us?" she asked sadly.

"I don't know," he answered simply, and looked down at the floor. "You were *very* important to me. Maybe I put you on a pedestal and I shouldn't have. People are human, after all, but you probably don't understand that."

"Yes, I do. You see, I made the mistake of falling in love with you."

"You don't know how much I wanted to hear those words a week ago," he said as he moved toward her.

"And now?"

"Now, maybe it's just a little late," he stated abruptly, then stopped as if he were jolted back to reality.

"At least I told you the truth. Doesn't that count for something?"

"Using my own words on me now," he accused.

"I just want you to be certain of what you're doing."

"I have my work cut out for me," he said, ignoring her words. "I'll check on Wilding's charities. And one thing you should know: I wasn't the one who drew up Ruth Klein's will. One of my associates did. I only delivered it so I could be at your building. I would have used any excuse to see you, even though I didn't know it that day."

"I don't understand," she replied, and then remembered his strange behavior that morning.

"I had some second thoughts about seeing you, I have to admit. I was getting in way over my head, and I wanted to be certain of my feelings for you. But, getting back to Wilding, you should have also remembered that my law firm only just recently started handling his affairs. So you see, my dear little detective, he used other lawyers to draw up those other wills," he told her condescendingly.

Instantly angered, Diane hissed, "I know that! When I went to the Surrogate's Court, the other law firm was written on the wills as plain as the nose on your face!"

The instant the words were out of her mouth, she realized her deadly mistake. And judging by the look in Brian's eyes, it hadn't escaped him.

"Ah, now the *real* truth comes out!" he raged.

164

"Now I know why you suddenly trust me—you *knew* I had nothing to do with the other wills!"

"It wasn't like that," she insisted.

"Why didn't you just come and ask me?"

"I just couldn't."

"Did you ever think that I might not have been the one who drew up the wills—I mean, before you did your little checking?" he interrogated.

"No, I never thought of that," she admitted glumly.

"There's a lot you never thought of."

"Brian, I love you and I made a mistake, but you don't have to nail me to the wall because of it. I told you I'm sorry . . . Or if I didn't, I meant to. It just comes down to how much you really care for me."

"Things aren't so black and white."

"No, I don't suppose they are, but I'm not going to let you make me feel guilty about something I've already punished myself enough for."

"I have to go."

"Typical. You talk about me taking the easy way out. Instead of staying here with me and working this out, you're going to run away."

"You don't even know what you've done, do you?" he asked in an incredulous voice.

"I made a mistake, that's all."

"It's much more than that. But I will deliver the facts. Don't worry about that," he promised, and turned sharply on his heel, walking in the direction of the door.

Diane watched as he strolled out of her apartment and out of her life. The man she loved was leaving her and she wanted to cry. But no tears would come. She felt too drained and numb even for that.

* * *

Diane somehow made it through the following day and the rest of the week. She didn't hear from Brian and wondered if he would keep his word and check into the charities Wilding had chosen. She thought he would, but the waiting was driving her up the wall.

One day, in the middle of the afternoon, as she sat at her desk, she got a call from Brian.

"I have what you want," he declared briskly, the moment she picked up the phone.

"What?"

"I said, I have the information you wanted on Wilding. Meet me downstairs at the bar," he ordered.

"But I'm in the middle of something," she muttered, totally taken aback.

"If you want the facts, I'll be waiting downstairs. It's up to you, but don't take all day," he said firmly, and then the line went dead.

Diane glared at the receiver, not believing he had actually hung up on her.

She wondered why he had sounded so angry. Perhaps he had found out that she was right about Wilding after all, and his ego couldn't take it. But then again, she admitted, maybe he had found out how foolish her accusations had been, and now he was really going to tell her off. Well, she would soon find out. As she walked to the elevator, she felt like a lamb being led to the slaughter, and the feeling wasn't at all pleasant.

Diane found Brian sitting alone at the bar. His head was bowed over his drink, making her feel that he wasn't too happy about what he was going to tell her. Suddenly she wished that they were meeting under different circumstances. She wanted to put her arms around him and hug him. She wanted to tell him how much she loved him and had missed him.

But happy endings only happened in fantasies, and she took a deep breath and steeled herself as she joined him at the bar.

"Hello, there," she said cheerfully, trying to dispel her anxiety.

He turned and looked up at her. Diane's heart ached and her stomach tightened. She was looking at the same blond hair and handsome features, but it was like looking at a stranger. The expression on his face was far from friendly, and his eyes had a glaze. Perhaps he had had too much to drink, she thought. She had hoped that time would have diluted some of the effect he had had on her. But taking in his beautiful eyes and his lips that had once touched her so intimately, she knew it had only been wishful thinking. And she cursed the weakness that allowed her to fall so easily under his spell.

"Hello, yourself," he replied nastily.

His harsh tone hurt her, and she found her strength crumbling. But she was determined to hold herself together; she was determined not to allow him to see the power he still held over her.

"How about buying me a drink?" she asked, trying her best to ignore his behavior.

"Sure, a celebration is in order. Name your poison."

"A white russian," she answered, and noted the muscle clenched along his jaw as he gave the bartender her order.

She remained silent, watching the bartender mix her drink.

"Cheers," she said when she finally had the glass in front of her.

"Cheers," he toasted grudgingly as he tapped his glass against hers.

"You sound like a sore loser," she ventured and sipped her drink.

"I guess you could put it that way. And knowing you, you would put it that way," he said. Then he threw back his head and downed the remainder of his drink.

"Well, I'm not here to be abused but to get the facts, as you would say. So, what's the information you have for me."

Brian sighed deeply and stared down at his empty glass. "Another one of these," he told the bartender.

"Haven't you had one too many already?" Diane asked calmly.

Ignoring her question, he said, "I did some checking on the charities. . . . And I hate to admit it, but you were right. Some of them are dummy corporations set up by Wilding."

"They are?" she asked, not bothering to hide her delight.

"Yeah, but don't rub it in," he replied sarcastically.

"Are you sure? I mean, how did you find out?" she went on excitedly.

"I have a friend in the attorney general's office, and he checked on them through his sources. All charities must be registered with the attorney general's office. And he found that they didn't have any record of the corporations as charities. It appears they were only shell corporations," he explained.

"What is a shell corporation?"

168

"It's a corporation that was legally created on paper but never operated. Then I examined the files in the Surrogate's Court and realized what he had done."

"But shouldn't the lawyer who drew up the wills have checked to make sure the charities were legitimate?"

"Not unless he had reason to believe the charities were phony. In each case, the widows were asked by their attorneys about the corporations, and the women all confirmed that they were definitely legal, tax-exempt corporations. So, the lawyers assumed there wasn't any reason to check further."

"Shouldn't the courts have known that something was fishy?"

"Wilding handled the estates proceedings *pro se.*"

"I see."

"Yes, he acted as his own attorney."

"I noticed there weren't any attorney's legal backs on any of the papers filed in the Surrogate's Court," Diane reported proudly.

"Smart girl. That's correct, and that's how he got away with it. A lawyer would have noticed something eventually. Wilding never reported the organizations as charities but as taxable corporations, and he paid any and all taxes that were due on the estates so nobody would know. And the attorney general's office was never put on notice of the proceedings, so they didn't even know anything about the estates and didn't have any reason to investigate."

"Clever. Well, what's the next step?" she asked enthusiastically.

"The next step is that the attorney general's office

will investigate to see if fraud has been committed," he answered, taking a sip of his fresh drink.

"And if they do?"

"Then Wilding will be charged with a crime."

"So where does this leave us?" she inquired, feeling triumphant.

"I don't know."

"You still can't hold that against me, that I thought you were involved."

He looked at her, then down at his martini.

"You still do," she declared in amazement.

"I need some time. I don't know."

"Brian, I can't believe you're willing to throw away what we meant to each other. I love you."

"Look, you got what you wanted. You got your facts," he stated coldly.

"But that's not *all* I wanted," she insisted.

"What else did you want?"

"I wanted to know that we had a future together."

"It's too late for that."

"I don't believe it."

"It's the principle of the thing," he told her, as if that were all the explanation she needed.

She stared at him, wondering how he could be so hardened. Suddenly she felt she had lost the war. It was all over. Tears threatened. Rather than let him gloat over his victory, she had to move. She wouldn't give the insensitive oaf the satisfaction of seeing her cry. Abruptly she slid off the bar stool and stood.

"Well, you can keep your damn principles, and I hope they make you happy!" she fumed, then exited the room quickly, tears streaming down her face.

The minute her feet hit the sidewalk, she felt like an

170

idiot. She had practically begged the man to take her back, and he had the nerve to throw his damn principles in her face. Well, he could just live with his principles. She hoped they'd keep him warm at night.

Not until hell freezes over would she ever make such a fool of herself again.

CHAPTER NINE

Time passed and Brian, true to his word, helped bring charges against Wilding. The renowned socialite had not been accused of killing any of the widows. No evidence of foul play could be found. The women had all died of natural causes, but most of the charities were found to be dummy corporations set up by Wilding.

It also came out that he had swindled money from his previous employer. In return for their not going public with his crime, Wilding had promised to pay the money back. At first he had tried gambling to regain the money, but instead he'd lost a great deal— including the remainder of his late wife's fortune. He was desperate for money. Then, when Wilding had learned that one of his neighbors was a wealthy elderly widow without any close relatives, he had seized upon the opportunity. He had quickly befriended her and persuaded her to allow him to be the executor of her will. Choosing the charities for the widow had been easy for the smooth-talking swindler. And so Wilding had discovered a good source of income for himself.

Sarah had been ecstatic about the news, and Diane was very happy for her. Sarah still insisted that Wilding had been involved with Ruthie's death, and it had been discovered that Wilding had been with her the morning she had died, but nothing could be proved. So Sarah had to be satisfied with the fact that the man was publicly exposed and charges were being brought against him. The chances were that he would never again be able to manipulate some lonely, unsuspecting person. Diane felt very good about this. Her boss had even helped her get a feature story on Wilding published, which was well received. But all that had happened did not make up for the fact that Wilding's demise had cost her Brian.

The more she thought about Brian, the angrier she got. How could he have given her up? She had told him the truth and had admitted her mistake. Didn't the guy have any room for forgiveness in his heart? It was hard to believe that anyone could be so unbending. He was a real fool, and she knew that someday he would wake up and be sorry. She only hoped it wouldn't be too late.

Finally Diane could no longer take the waiting and decided to pick up the phone and call him. She could at least congratulate him for his part in bringing a swindler to justice. That would be a good enough excuse to get him on the phone, at least, she thought.

Diane called him, but he wasn't in his office. She left a message that she would like him to call her back. The day passed and she didn't hear from him.

Later the following day, she still hadn't heard from him. She thought that perhaps her message had somehow been misplaced, and he had never received it. It was hard for her to believe that he wouldn't at least return her phone call. So she called him again, and again his secretary said that he was out. Suddenly Diane wondered if he had instructed his secretary that he didn't want to take any calls from Diane. She left another message for him to call her.

Two days passed and she still hadn't heard from him. Now she had to admit that he must be trying to avoid her. This infuriated Diane. He could have at least made one lousy call! He hadn't even known the reason she had telephoned him. What if she were in some kind of serious trouble? What if she were dying? She knew she was getting a little melodramatic, but she now knew a cad when she saw him!

He had said he loved her. Could he turn his feelings on and off like a water faucet? She had a good mind to go and hang out in front of his apartment building and give him a dose of his own medicine. But, no, Diane decided she wouldn't stoop to his level. *It was just too low!* If he wanted her out of his life, then she would oblige him.

She finally came to the conclusion that she had to forget about Brian and get her life back together. With this thought firmly embedded in her mind, Diane walked toward her apartment. To her surprise, then annoyance, Brian was standing in front of her building.

His hair was unruly as he lounged casually up against a wall. Her heart leapt to her throat and her legs felt like they would give out from under her. She hated herself for still being so affected by this man who couldn't care less whether she lived or died.

"Up to your old tricks. Waiting for a pickup, I see," she said sarcastically, and sped past him into the building.

"Diane!" he called, but she continued on her way.

She stopped at her mailbox, her body shaking from

anger. Did he think he could pop up at her door just because he decided he wanted something? Did he really believe she'd be available? Well, Mr. Scott had another thing coming! she thought.

"Diane, I want to talk to you," he began, suddenly standing next to her. Then he touched her shoulder.

She spun around to face him. "I think this is where you came in, isn't it?" she said coldly. "What do you want to talk about?"

"Isn't there somewhere we can go and be alone?"

"That is, if *I* wanted to be alone with you. Why should I? You didn't even have the decency to return my phone calls!"

"You're right, and I'm sorry. I should have called, and there's no excuse for my not doing so. But I needed time to sort things out."

"Don't tell me you're apologizing?"

"Diane, if you're angry, I can't blame you."

"Angry! Oh, I'm not angry, Brian. What made you think that?" she nearly shouted.

"I can see there's no reasoning with you . . ."

"I suppose you thought you could just lurk around my apartment, and I'd be so happy to see you that I'd just fall into your arms. Sorry to disappoint you, Mr. Presumptuous," she snapped.

"You sound very bitter."

"You bet I am!" she shot back. "Now, if you don't mind, I have plans for this evening and I'm late," she informed him coolly, then turned and made a dash toward the opened elevator doors.

"Boy, you don't waste any time!" he said sarcastically as she stepped into the waiting car.

The door slammed shut, and Diane felt like a chapter of her life had just been closed.

She had not heard any of the words she wanted to hear—nothing about loving her, about missing her, about building a future with her. All he had said was that he had to sort things out. Did he really think that they could pick up where they had left off?

She didn't have any plans for this evening yet, but the night was still young. Her life had been put on hold, and now it was about time she got back to the real world.

Brian stood in the lobby dumbfounded. He had expected her to be a little angry with him, but he had not been prepared for the spitfire he had encountered.

So he hadn't returned her phone calls, he thought. Big deal! What had she expected after the way she had treated him? That he was just supposed to forgive and forget? A man's mind simply didn't work that way. It wasn't that uncomplicated. Well, one thing was for certain: he wasn't going to beg, he decided, and walked out of the building.

Diane reached her apartment and slammed the door shut behind her. She felt absolutely miserable—the worst ever. Why did she have to see him? Seeing him had only reminded her of how much she really loved him. Mentally she had accepted that he was a rat, but emotionally she was still very much tied to him. It was so hard for her to believe that someone who had touched her soul so completely wouldn't be the man she was destined to spend the rest of her life with.

She tried to console herself, but she couldn't. From

day one, their relationship had been like a volcano about to erupt. They never had a chance. And all her talk about forgetting him and getting her life back together had been for naught. She still loved him, more than ever. She couldn't kid herself any longer. He was a part of her and always would be.

She glanced around her apartment and wondered what she would do with herself tonight. She could call up one of her girlfriends but decided she didn't want to inflict her morose mood on any of them.

Disheartened, she plopped down on the sofa.

Suddenly her doorbell rang, startling her. Brian! she thought, and jumped to her feet.

As she walked to the door conflicting emotions warred within her.

"I'll be right there," she said.

So certain it was Brian, she didn't even bother to look through the peephole and turned the lock. She swung the door open, and there stood the cherub-faced Sarah Dempsey.

Diane's face dropped.

"Did I catch you at a bad moment?" the woman asked, noticing Diane's disappointment.

"I'm sorry, Sarah. I thought you were someone else," Diane explained. "I'm happy to see you're back. Please come in."

"I won't stay long if you're expecting someone," Sarah told her apologetically as she followed Diane into the living room.

"You can stay as long as you like. I'm not expecting anyone. I mean, I'm no longer expecting anyone. It was only wishful thinking on my part," Diane said, a sadness creeping into her voice.

"Sounds like troubles of the heart," Sarah declared wisely, eyeing Diane.

"Yes, you're right about that," Diane admitted, and forced a smile. "Please sit down," she offered as she led the woman to her sofa.

Once Sarah was settled on the cushioned seat, Diane asked, "Would you like some coffee or tea?"

"No, thanks, dear. I just wanted to let you know I was home and that all my friends just *loved* your article," she said, her eyes brightening.

"Thank you."

"Brian was impressed, too?" the old woman asked.

Sarah was watching Diane too closely, giving her the feeling that the old woman knew there was trouble in paradise.

"No, as a matter of fact, he never even mentioned it to me," Diane admitted.

"You had a falling out?" Sarah asked bluntly.

Diane nodded as tears threatened.

"I'm sorry for asking. Just an old woman butting in where she shouldn't. But somehow I feel that I might be responsible."

"No, you're not. What made you think that?" Diane asked, pulling herself together.

"We'll, everything was all right with the two of you before all of that Wilding stuff came up. It has to do with that man, doesn't it?"

Diane smiled. Sarah had that angry tone in her voice the way she always did whenever she had mentioned Wilding.

"Brian still holds it against me that I thought he was involved," Diane explained.

"That young whippersnapper. I don't know what's

178

with these men today. Doesn't he know what a prize you are?" she asked affectionately.

"Apparently not," Diane answered with a little laugh.

"Well, at least you can laugh. That's a good start. Don't worry, Diane. He'll be back. If the man really loves you, he'll be back."

"How do I know if he really loves me?"

"It's not what he says but what he does that is important," she answered, raising her index finger in the air.

Diane thought this little woman could probably teach her a thing or two about men.

"It's really good to see you, Sarah," she said warmly.

"Have you eaten?" Sarah asked.

"No, I haven't," Diane admitted.

"Don't ever neglect your health, Diane," Sarah warned.

"You're right."

"I'm going to treat you to a really nice dinner," the woman declared, and got to her feet.

"That's very nice of you, but—"

"No buts about it. I'm taking you out, and that's all there is to it. You don't want Brian coming back to find you a skeleton of your former self."

"No, we can't have that. But you're not buying—I am."

"We'll see about that!" Sarah exclaimed, and started toward the door.

Diane laughed. She was happy to see her friend and felt better already. Sarah had been right: laughter was the best medicine for a broken heart.

There would be a lot of pain to get through in the days ahead, but she would handle it. She loved Brian and doubted whether she would ever love anyone more. But she was a survivor, and she would make it. After all, she had good friends like Sarah Dempsey to make sure she did.

Brian had not wanted to beg, but as the days passed he was about ready to do anything to put an end to his misery. Everything was going wrong. His life was a mess. He had even spent a few days sick in bed with the flu! For an active man like Brian that was a fate worse than death. He swore he would never see Diane again. She had been nothing but trouble since day one. But no matter how much he tried to convince himself he was better off without her, Brian knew that he didn't want to live his life if she was not a part of it. It was the hardest thing in the world for him to admit, but he was lost without her.

And as he had time to think about their relationship, he knew that his not forgiving Diane had more to do with his own insecurity than with anything she might have done. He loved her, but he had been terribly hurt by her. He had never given himself over so completely to another human being before, and he didn't want to take the risk of doing that again. The cost had been too high. He had experienced the power of love, and he had been left with a broken heart. The power she held over him was too frightening. He had been like putty in her hands.

But he loved her, and he wanted to spend the rest of his life with her. He missed her beautiful eyes, the sound of her voice, the touch of her satiny skin. And he knew he could no longer afford to sit around and nurse his bruised and terrified ego. He had to talk to her. He had to win her back, or his life wouldn't be worth anything. He hadn't even been able to work, and he had always loved his work. He had often thought something was wrong with him because he had enjoyed his work so much. Finally Brian had to admit that he would be in big trouble if she didn't take him back.

Diane made sure that she kept busy. She lined up dates with her friends weeks in advance, just so she wouldn't sit home alone. She was on the go so much that she didn't have too much time to think about him. Eventually she began to feel like she was getting her life back together.

Her friends had all been supportive, and she realized how much she had missed spending time with them. She went out to dinners, to parties, and caught up on all the recent movies. She stayed out as late as she could as often as she could so that when she came home, she just fell into bed. She knew that someday soon the whirlwind would have to stop, but it was getting her through the pain, and that's what she needed at the moment.

But one evening Diane suddenly found herself at home without anything to do. A girlfriend had called at the last minute to cancel their date, because her father was ill.

There was a good movie on television, so she turned it on and went into the kitchen to see what she had in the refrigerator to eat. But as she neared the room the phone rang and she turned back toward the living room to answer it.

The minute she placed the receiver to her ear, she heard the sound of traffic in the background.

"Hello," she said.

There was no response.

"Hello," she repeated.

"Hello," came a voice.

It was Brian! Butterflies flitted in the pit of her stomach.

"Where are you?" she asked, too stunned to think of anything better to say.

"On the street corner."

Diane's heart melted. She wanted to be in his arms, but she knew she couldn't.

"What do you want?" she asked coldly, suddenly reminding herself of the pain he had put her through.

"How about supper?"

"I'm not hungry."

"I want to see you."

"I'm busy."

"We have to talk," he insisted.

"I've heard that before."

"Can I buy you something to eat?" he asked in a boyish voice.

Diane hesitated. She wanted to be with him and yet she didn't want to compromise herself.

"Please see me, so I can tell you how sorry I am. I was a jerk and I admit it."

"I'm glad you're finally admitting it."

She was starting to weaken and she steeled herself, afraid to see him again, afraid that nothing would come of their meeting except that her wound would be opened once again.

"I don't know . . ." she finally managed.

"I love you, Diane."

"I love you, too, but that didn't seem to be enough."

"I don't want to live my life without you," he said with emotion.

Diane couldn't deny that she felt the same and suddenly knew that nothing else mattered except being with Brian.

"Just tell me where I should meet you!" she exclaimed.

They agreed to meet at a little Italian restaurant close by, and as she walked into the place, her knees buckled and her stomach flip-flopped. She was going to see the man she loved, and her destiny was in his hands. Would her future be filled with bright promise, or would she be sentenced to a life of darkness?

Once she entered the restaurant, a waiter quickly approached her and pointed her in the direction of Brian's table. Her legs felt like lead weights as she moved slowly across the room.

The minute she saw Brian's haggard appearance, her heart went out to him.

"What happened to you? You look awful," she declared without thinking as she seated herself across from him.

"Thanks, I needed that," he said sadly.

"I'm sorry. It's just that I'm worried about you," she explained softly, and extended her hand across the table to him.

He took her hand into his and squeezed it gently.

"I've missed the touch of your skin," he murmured affectionately.

"That's not all I've missed," she retorted playfully.

Brian grinned. His smile warmed her and sent her pulses racing.

"What are we going to do?" he asked abruptly in a more somber tone.

"I don't know. I know that I love you, but I don't know if that's enough."

"I love you, too."

Suddenly a waiter appeared at their table and asked, "Can I get you something to drink?"

Diane looked over at Brian's drink, a glass of white wine, and replied, "I'll have one of those."

The man quickly nodded and disappeared.

"I think we should get married," Brian said suddenly.

"What?" she asked, not believing her ears.

"I'm not such a bad catch."

"No, you're not a bad catch at all," she agreed, "but, Brian, we have a lot of things to work out."

"Like what?" he asked in a very charming way.

"Don't give me that little-boy routine," she said. "You know what I'm talking about."

He stared at her and remained silent.

"What about truth and honesty, the ingredients you said were missing from our relationship?" she asked directly.

"You would have to bring that up."

"Yes, Brian, I do. I think it's important for us to get everything out in the open, because otherwise I really don't know if we can have a future together."

"It wasn't that you shouldn't have brought it up,

Diane. It's just that it's very difficult for me to admit that I . . ."

"Please go on."

"That I was frightened of you," he confessed, then quickly took another sip of his wine.

"I don't understand."

"Of course you don't. It's just that you had so much power over me—that's why I wouldn't forgive you about Wilding. By suspecting me of being involved in his scam, you stripped away some of my integrity as well. Everything about you was dashing my well-organized life to pieces. Does that make any sense?"

"I'm not sure."

"I was hurt, terribly hurt, and I had never before experienced that kind of pain. At first, I went through all kinds of wild jealousy attacks because I really thought you were involved with someone else and weren't telling me. And I had never been jealous in my life. Do you know what that does to a man's ego?"

He cocked his head and arched his brows, and an incredulous look crossed his face, emphasizing his point.

Diane couldn't help but laugh.

"I'm sorry," she said quickly, "but it was just the expression on your face."

"It's okay. I can laugh about it now, too. Otherwise, I wouldn't be able to tell you about it. I guess what I'm trying to say is that I'm not perfect—I'm not one hundred percent—but I'm willing to work at a marriage with you. I want you to be with me, and I want you to share my life with me. And maybe, at times, I'm not the easiest person to get along with, but I love you."

Diane smiled slightly.

"I hope you feel the same way," he said in a low voice.

Just then the waiter interrupted and placed Diane's drink on the table in front of her.

"Thank you," she murmured, and the waiter nodded his appreciation before he walked away.

Diane looked down at her wine glass and then looked back into Brian's face.

"All of a sudden I'm not very hungry. What do you say we go back to my place and hold each other?" she asked with the glow of love sparkling in her eyes.

"I thought you'd never ask," Brian replied with a delighted chuckle.

"I've missed you so much," she whispered.

"Not as much as I've missed you. And I can't wait to hold you in my arms and kiss your sweet, sensuous lips," he told her softly with warmth and longing ringing through his voice.

Brian signaled the waiter and paid the bill.

Once out onto the sidewalk, they walked silently, hand in hand, quickly making their way to Diane's apartment. A full moon loomed between two tall buildings. Diane's heart swelled. The moon was a good omen. It blessed their golden journey.

As her door closed out the rest of the world, Brian took her into the security of his arms. It was like coming home again as her body nestled against his. He cupped her chin tenderly in his warm hand. His eager lips swooped down upon hers, claiming them for himself. Her eyes involuntarily shut and Diane abandoned herself to the passion she had thought she would always have to live without. A kaleidoscope of metallic blue and silver illuminated her vision. The hunger of his soft lips was thrilling, and a sense of warmth and serenity enveloped her.

His kiss was slow and thoughtful and meant everything to her—the sky, the stars, and more. It was pure ecstasy, transporting her on a soft and wispy cloud.

Brian suddenly raised his mouth from hers, gazed into her eyes, and whispered, "I love you, darling. Please don't ever leave me again."

Diane stared into his dark, misty eyes, framed by his long lashes, and knew all the love she wanted was there. She no longer doubted that he would be the man she would spend the rest of her life with.

"I won't ever," she promised.

Her words were smothered by his lips as his mouth recaptured hers, sealing their ultimate possession of each other. They were one. It was a kiss of beginning.

If you liked *Romancing the Stone,* you'll <u>love</u>

THE PEREGRINE CONNECTION

Romantic suspense novels for women who enjoy action, danger, mystery, and intrigue mixed up in their romances.

_____ #1 TALONS OF THE FALCON   18498-3-36
_____ #2 FLIGHT OF THE RAVEN   12560-X-24
_____ #3 IN SEARCH OF THE DOVE 11038-6-12

by Rebecca York   **$2.95 each**